Praise for *The O*

GU00566768

"It has been a long time since a novel captivated me to such an extent [...] Written with wisdom and compassion, it will resonate long after the last page is turned."

– Karina M Szczurek in *Cape Times*

"I haven't had an 'unputdownable' book in a while – this is it!"

– Lorraine Sithole, Chairperson of Bookworms Book Club

"As a woman, *The Ones with Purpose* hit me on so many levels. Jele skillfully weaves together a number of themes that represent the reality of many women's lives: joys and pains of motherhood; bonds of sisterhood; patriarchy; journeying the sick to the grave; living with deep hurt and trauma."

– Dr Lulu Gwagwa

"The writing in this heartbreaking novel is nothing short of impeccable."

– Nondumiso Tshabangu, Editor of *Africa's Lit*

"Woven within these stories of how family tragedy compounds on itself, like negative interest, are larger questions, national in nature and spanning generations."

– Mbali Sikakana in *The Johannesburg Review of Books*

NOZIZWE CYNTHIA JELE

THE ONES WITH PURPOSE

Kwela Books

KWELA Books,
an imprint of NB Publishers,
a division of Media24 Boeke (Pty) Ltd
40 Heerengracht, Cape Town, South Africa
PO Box 879, Cape Town, South Africa, 8000
www.kwela.com

Cover photo: Shutterstock/moj0j0
Cover design by Michiel Botha
Typography by Nazli Jacobs
Set in 11 on 16pt Linux Libertine

solutions
Printed by **novus print**, a Novus Holdings company

First edition, first impression 2018
Second impression 2018

ISBN: 978-0-7957-0843-5
ISBN: 978-0-7957-0844-2 (epub)
ISBN: 978-0-7957-0845-9 (mobi)

To dad.
You're in our hearts.
Always.

For women with cancer who have
found their fire, and for those who are still searching.

– Elizabeth Berg, *Talk Before Sleep*

home is better than
this place

I imagined a dying person's last breath as something resembling an exclamation mark, distinct and hanging mid-air like an interrupted thought. My older sister Fikile's last breath before she dies is nothing of the sort. There is no rattling noise at the back of her throat. No relentless twitching. No clinging to life. Fikile dies with no more fuss than a switch of a light bulb.

*   *   *

I wake before the unforgiving December sun rises fast and fierce, before T-Bone starts howling and chasing his own shadow. People on the radio and television have said it is one of the hottest summers the country has seen in a while. Government officials have pleaded with the people to stay hydrated and keep the festivities indoors – a call unheeded by the residents of New Hope township, who go about spending their hard-earned year-end bonuses and savings. Smoke arises from braais and weddings and traditional ceremonies at every second house. Radios boom full blast with the latest House and Afro-pop music, and the children skip rope and kick tattered leather soccer balls and merrily suck on ice pops, leaving their mouths in varying shades of blue and red and purple. Even those whose dreams had perished in what was undeniably a bad year, a testing year, swallow their failures, collect their pride, put on brave smiles and join in the merriment. Of the heat, Ma said this year's is as if the air was cooked first before being released. Miraculously people know how to breathe in it.

I lift the thin, white sheet, climb out of bed to brush my teeth and wash my face. I move quietly so as not to wake Sizwe next to me, unperturbed by the heat, his crescendo of snores sending tiny vibrations across the room. It is a wonder to me how, with his leanness and good health, Sizwe manages to create such a disturbance. I envy him though, for his ability to sleep through a crisis. I have managed no more than a couple of hours' sleep since we brought Fikile back home from the hospital two days before.

For good this time.

When we last took Fikile to New Hope Hospital, Sister Luthuli, whom I know from the years of coming in and out of the emergency room, pulled me aside. This was after Fikile had come down with a fever that left her hot and cold from night sweats, her body drenched, and pain palpable in her twitched lip. Even Ma's trusted mud-brown concoction of indistinguishable roots, chillies, lemon, garlic and honey had not been enough to break the fever. Her breathing was so shallow, as if the fever was feeding off it.

"She won't get better, not here anyway." Sister Luthuli said, not impolitely, that there was nothing the hospital could do for my sister at that stage. It wasn't the first time she had told me this, preparing me for the worst. "Best to take her home and keep her warm and comfortable. I'll give you something for her to take to numb the pain."

"She's not breathing properly, I can't take her home, not like this," I protested. "We don't know what to do. I'm asking you to keep her for a few days until the fever subsides, please."

"Anele, what I'm trying to say is, today your sister has a fever and shortness of breath, tomorrow she will have difficulties swallowing, and a day after that something else. Are you going to rush her here each time? Just look at her." Sister Luthuli pointed at Fikile with her eyes. "She doesn't deserve this treatment. Please Anele, let Fikile spend the last of her days surrounded by people she loves."

I refused to look at my sister, instead stared the other away. A turbulent motion rose through my cheeks, settling behind my eyelids, hot and wet. I swallowed my saliva.

"Fikile's body cannot cope anymore and there is nothing we can do for her. As much as this is hard to accept, the worst is almost over for you, and for her," Sister Luthuli continued, exasperated. "This can't be easy for her either. I know it is hard, especially for the children to see their mother like this. I went through the same with my husband. In the end, I decided to let him come home and die in the care of people who loved him, in the house he built, and the bed he slept on for years. It was the hardest decision I ever had to make, but I have no regrets," she paused as if to select the words in her mind, "home is better than this place." She squeezed my shoulder lightly before walking away.

A few minutes later another nurse appeared and wheeled my sister away. I turned to Sizwe and held him tight.

Sister Luthuli's words played in my mind; I couldn't sleep. The following morning I brought Fikile back home.

*   *   *

From my bedroom to Fikile's room at the end of the narrow hallway, I pass Ma's bedroom which she shares with her grandchildren. I picture the children, my daughter, Mvula, and nephew Bafana, piled on Ma's queen-size bed, sagging in the middle from the years of use, and my niece, Lesihle, sprawled on the small mattress on the floor, exhausted from the previous day's play. School let out earlier in the week; it will be another month before they reopen. The children were starting to complain of boredom. I hear the familiar murmurs of Ma's morning prayers peppered with muffled sobs and careful nose blows. Ma cries a lot during her prayers these days, such that later when she joins me for tea, her face is mushy and raw as if she was up all night fighting invisible monsters. Prayers are her new habit. After more than a two-decade-long church absence, Ma woke up one day, shortly after Fikile's diagnosis, and walked to Reverend Madida's house. From then on, every Sunday, she dressed Mvula and waited for Fikile to take them to church. She started adorning herself with the black and purple cloth worn by the church elderlies, and attending Bible studies and prayer meetings with the women of prayer. She returned to society, the same society that had chewed and spat her out and left her in a black hole for years. Old friendships were rekindled; aunties who were present in our childhood but had not set foot in our house in years, and who, when they bumped into me or my siblings at the supermarket, in church or on the streets, looked at us with sharp embarrassment, once more began to make regular appearances. They told Ma how proud they were of her for bravely tackling the devil by his horns. They denounced alcohol, and in their high-pitched voices declared a new war on this destroyer of families.

Fikile's bedroom door is a crack open.

"Fiks, are you up? It's me, Anele," I whisper as I walk in. My senses had long adjusted to the darkness and lingering scents of camphor and death. Fikile's eyes are closed, but her moans suggest she is not asleep. "Did you get some sleep?" I lean over, touch her forehead and gently plant a kiss. Her ashen, paper-thin skin feels cool to my lips. I open the blanket and run my hand over the sheet, relieved to find it dry. "How are you feeling, are you in pain?"

Fikile slowly opens her eyes, moves her head slightly up and down, and parts her lips.

I bend over expectantly. I would give anything to hear my sister's voice again. Fikile last constructed a sentence several weeks back, and even then it was nothing more than a whisper of her children's names in the order she had brought them into the world – Khanya, Lesihle, and Bafana.

"What is it?" I lean closer. Fikile's body has shrunk into

itself under the blanket, leaving an outline, an approximation of the woman she once was.

Fikile starts to babble impatiently.

"*Shh*, okay, don't say anything. I'll get your medicines and something to eat. Will you try today?"

Fikile shuts her eyes. A lone tear rolls down her cheek, collects at her collarbone.

"Oh, you can just try, sisi, you don't have to force yourself." I wipe her face with the back of my hand.

I leave Fikile's room in haste and close the door gently behind me. I move to the kitchen where I fill the kettle with water, and put it to boil to prepare sour soft porridge for everyone. I stand there transfixed, watching the bubbles from the glass kettle form slowly at the base and rise and pop. I feel parts of my body burst along with each bubble. The kettle snaps shut and stops.

I don't hear Ma walk in.

"I dreamt of your father again." She pulls out a chair and sits hunched over the table, her hands on her head. She does not look up when she speaks. "He was wiggling his finger as if trying to tell me something. His lips were moving but his voice was not there. I tried to tell him I couldn't hear, but each time I moved closer to him he stepped back until he was only a figure on a horizon."

"It's only a dream, Ma. You're tired."

I pour water in the pan and stir in maize meal until the mixture is thick and smooth. After a few minutes, I lower the heat on the stove and make us tea.

"After all this time, I still sense your father's disappointment." Ma looks up, gives me the most direct look through her one good eye. Ma's eyes are sunken in their sockets as if Fikile's illness is also hers. "Do you blame me too?"

"Ma –"

"Do you? Because I know your brother hates me, your sister too, though she tries to hide it. I know deep down in her heart I'm nothing to her." Ma begins to tremble in her seat. "You do," she says, hurt when I do not respond. "My children hate me."

"We don't hate you, Ma."

"Then why does it feel that way? I should have followed your father a long time ago."

"Your tea will get cold."

Ma looks at me, and down at the table as if only then noticing the tea in front of her. She pushes the cup away, shakes her head.

"You need some energy, Ma."

She turns her eyes towards Fikile's room. We sit for a while not speaking, each drowning in guilt – why is it Fikile dying in the room next door? I lift my cup and try to sip, but the tea has turned tepid. I take both cups over to the sink and empty them. I stir the porridge one more time and turn off the stove. I pour a little for Fikile and for Ma, sprinkle sugar and add milk to both.

"I doubt she will eat. She can't even open her eyes."

"How is she going to regain her strength if she refuses to eat?" Ma says, drying her eyes with the handkerchief, soggy and crumpled from all the crying. She follows me to Fikile's room.

My mother rejects any notion that her eldest daughter will not overcome her illness and be well again. She carries this unwavering hope in her demeanour – head slightly bowed, lips stubbornly pressed – as we rejoice over small feats: Fikile sipping mouthfuls of water, making a gesture with her hand, lifting an eyelid, or when a flush of colour returns to her skin. My mother's resolution pokes guilt at my conscience for not giving my sister a chance, for murdering her the day she received the results of her first mammogram showing a marble-sized lumpy mess in her left breast.

We sit on either side of the bed, me trying to feed my sister, and Ma forcing her own porridge down her throat in an exaggerated and illustrative manner meant to divert Fikile's attention from the food. It is a trick she used with us as children when we were sick and refused to eat, something she had learned as a domestic worker and nanny years before she gave birth to her own children. It is a trick she believes can still do the job. Fikile refuses to open her mouth, and turns her face away.

"We will try again later," I say. Fikile hasn't eaten since we brought her home.

Doctor Thusi had warned us about the lack of appetite in dying people. He said it wasn't uncommon, and the worst thing we could do is shove food down Fikile's throat.

I fill up a small washing basin with warm water, remove

Fikile's diaper, and start to wipe her body with a soft cloth. Her muscles begin to relax. Her face is almost in a dream-like state as I run the cloth over her cheeks, forehead, neck, under her emaciated arms, between her legs. She smiles, or her face contorts into an expression resembling a smile; I can't help but smile too. When I'm finished, I rub pepper-mint and lavender oils all over her body to relieve pain. The essential oils were recommended by a sales assistant at the organic shop in town. I dress Fikile in her favourite night-dress, white with black lace trims – the lace tearing in places with wear – and cover her with a light blanket. Fikile bought the nightdress the day we went for her bra fitting post the mastectomy. She said she was still a woman and deserved to feel like one. Fikile falls asleep immediately after her bath. I rub a wet swab over her lips and apply Lesihle's straw-berry gloss. I stand back, happy with my work.

"You should have been a nurse," Ma says. "You are good with people."

Ma and I drift back to the kitchen.

"You must call your brother-in-law again. It is not right that he has not been to see his wife for so long," Ma says. "How does he thinks she feels?"

"Your son-in-law only thinks about himself. He doesn't care that his wife is lying here dying. Is it necessary to call him? If he wants to see Fikile, he will come. I don't have the energy to run around after a grown man telling him what to do. You call him."

I could count on my hands the number of times Thiza has

checked on his wife and the children since they moved in with us several months ago at Ma's insistence, after Fikile's cancer progressed to her lungs, leaving her short of breath. Thiza had packed up Fikile and the children and brought them to our house that very afternoon. He did not stay long enough to see them settle in, his relief evident.

"Please, Anele," Ma says, ignoring my outpour. "Please call him."

"He won't pick up anyway," I say begrudgingly as I dial my brother-in-law's number.

I am wrong, Thiza answers his phone. I tell him Ma wants him to come see Fikile.

"I'll try," Thiza says as if I asked him to swing by the shops to buy bread and butter.

"Try what? Just come. She is not getting better." I hang up before he responds. "Please don't make me call him again."

I would be lying if I say I know when the pleasantries between Thiza and I faded, replaced by strained tolerance. For the longest time, we have moved around each other with practised care, fully aware of what lies beneath the pretence.

"You must exercise patience with him. You're not the only one suffering," Ma says.

I could smack Ma for insinuating that Thiza cares; instead I walk out of the kitchen.

Sizwe is awake, dressing to get ready for work. I am once again relieved that I could take my festive season leave early to help Ma care for Fikile and the children.

"How is she?" Sizwe asks.

"She still won't eat, but at least her temperature has dropped."

He comes over and puts his arms around me. I rest my cheek on his shoulder. The material of his overalls feels scratchy and hard on my skin. I'm comforted.

"What am I going to do if Fikile dies?" I whisper to him. "I'm scared."

"*Shh*, don't think that way," Sizwe says.

I close my eyes, ashamed. I am killing my sister again.

* * *

Throughout the day Ma and I take turns to sit with Fikile. We feed her again, or attempt to feed her. We fill her in on the latest developments in our household, the latest gossip from the stokvel ladies, some of whom have come to check on her, and the progress of the new church building that, according to Ma, looks like one is already entering heaven. I don't know if Fikile hears us but we speak to her anyway.

After dinner, we bring the children in to see her. Bafana has the most questions. "Is Ma going to open her eyes? Why does she sleep the whole day? Will Ma play with me again? Where is Dad? I want Dad."

My daughter, Mvula, who is not yet four years old, tugs at the hem of my dress, staring at her aunt without speaking. Later, she finds me alone in the kitchen, latches onto my leg like a tick and says in a small, cracked voice that she doesn't want me to get sick.

Lesihle sits quietly at the top of the bed, next to her

mother's head, her face full of unshed tears. When it is time for them to go to bed, Lesihle asks to spend a few more minutes alone with her mother. I hear soft sobs behind me as I close the door. My eyes prickle.

Sizwe comes home soon after the children are in bed. I let him wash off the grease and heat, and, after a few moments with Fikile, bring him a plate of food and a beer. We sit on the veranda not saying much. Only after midnight does Sizwe lead me inside the house to our room. I stop in Fikile's room, lean over her bed to check her breath. Satisfied, I turn her body, and watch her sleep in her morphine-induced state. In bed, Sizwe takes my hand in his and kisses my forehead. He closes his eyes and falls asleep.

Three hours later, my eyes push open.

I slip out of our bedroom into Fikile's room, find a space next to her and lie still. Lying next to my sister reminds me of when we were younger and the roaring thunderstorms would wake me from sleep, dazed and panicked. I would leave my single bed and crawl into Fikile's next to mine. My sister would groan, spread herself across the bed, covering every inch of space and in her sleepy voice tell me to grow up and get off, that the lightning was far away and could not hurt me. I didn't believe her, and would push and beg until she made room for me. She would tell me not to touch her, that she didn't need extra heat. Of course it was impossible for our bodies not to rub; still I would sleep on the edge and will myself not to move, intent on pleasing my sister, and grateful for her small mercies.

I wake up with a jerk an hour or so later. Fikile is dead.

Because I cannot believe that my sister is gone – shouldn't she have sent a signal, a warning, stirred some drama of sorts? – I lean over, holding my breath, watching intently for the movement of the blanket covering her body. I run my fingers over her face, feeling the thin skin along her cheek bones, prominent and sharp from the ravages of her illness. I place my index and third finger under her jaw right next to the windpipe and press lightly. No sign of life there either. Eventually I pull back to steady the quivers shooting through my body, blood pounding in my head, my mouth cold and too numb to call for help.

*   *   *

It is a while before I leave Fikile's dead body and step over into the narrow corridor towards Ma's bedroom. I tap once, let myself inside. In the dark I make out her silhouette, on her knees beside the bed. Ma does not look up. She continues to pray, harder, faster. The sound comes from a deep place in her body and squeezes out of her through her throat, pained and coarse. I expect the children to wake up, cranky, disturbed from their sleep; no one stirs. I remain standing for another minute, then gently shut the door behind me, and go to wake Sizwe. He sits on the edge of the bed, elbows on his thighs, head in his hands, his body shaking. I sit next to him and bury my face against his chest.

The first call I make is to Doctor Thusi. He answers his phone on the first ring, like someone who is prepared for action; a combat soldier. If he was sleeping, he does not give any signs. I inform him of Fikile's passing. Doctor Thusi is mute for a moment. I fear I may have to repeat myself. As I open my mouth, he speaks, his voice clear and steady from years of counselling and healing. He tells me he will come straightaway.

I proceed to call members of my family. Auntie Betty swallows her heartache in a single sigh and promises to catch the first taxi to our house. Auntie Ntombi sobs on the phone and asks me over and over to say it isn't so, until I hang up on her just as she is calling one of my cousins to come to the phone to help her understand what has just happened to her niece. My younger brother, Mbuso, answers on the third ring. I only say: "It's Fikile."

"I'll be there before noon," he says in the quietest tone.

Thiza's phone goes straight to voicemail.

"He switches off his phone at night; obviously, he doesn't want his whores to disturb him when he's pretending to be a family man," Fikile once said. I don't leave a message. Ma suggests that Sizwe drives over to Thiza's house to find him. It's a pointless mission, both Sizwe and I know he won't find him there, but neither of us have the heart to tell Ma. So Sizwe drives to Thiza and Fikile's house in the other section of the township to tell him his wife has died.

My father's younger brother, Uncle Majaha, does not pick up his phone, and after a familiar recording of a baritone voice commands the caller to "Khuluma" – a crude message as Ma has pointed out to my amused uncle on several occasions – I leave a message: Fikile is gone. My father's older sister, Auntie Nomzamo, asks me to pray with her for Fikile's soul. She prays to the Lord Jesus Christ of Nazareth, the Father, and the Holy Spirit, the Almighty, the Alpha and Omega, the King of Kings. She prays until my right ear is hot and buzzes. My phone battery dies and that marks the end of our conversation.

"Is she coming?" Ma asks.

"We got cut off. Why wouldn't she?"

"I never know with your aunt, that woman never liked me from day one." She wants to say more, but her voice does not let her. Instead she swallows, sighs. "We shall see."

"She will come, Ma. Fikile is – was – their child. This is not about you or Aunt Nomzamo."

I'm numb from making all the calls. We agree to contact the remaining family members later in the day.

* * *

Half an hour later Sizwe returns without Thiza but with Maria, our neighbour and family friend. We call her Auntie Maria. The look of disappointment at not seeing Thiza is evident on Ma's face, she does not say anything. Auntie Maria is distracting her with sobs. A pink satin nightdress shows underneath Auntie Maria's loose blue pinafore, the red doek is skewed on her head. Waves of tremors like small earthquakes spread from her chest and shoulders and roll down to her layered belly. When she gets closer to Ma, she flings herself down in front of her, bellowing: "Fikile! Why leave us?

23

Why?" This goes on for a while, until Ma, who has been swallowing her tears, lets them pour out.

Sizwe turns briefly to me, pleading with his eyes: *do something*. I shake my head. Ma maintains that when people come to pay their respects to the aggrieved family it is rarely about the deceased; she says people are there to mourn their past personal losses, and that as an aggrieved family it is important to keep your grief in check and not to get caught up in other people's emotional tangles. I am convinced now that Auntie Maria is weeping for her dead husband.

In her own time, Auntie Maria rises from the floor and takes a seat next to Ma.

"I don't know what to say," she speaks with a voice full of grief. "I just don't know."

"We are waiting for the hearse, Doctor Thusi is also on his way," Ma says with regained composure.

I have known Auntie Maria since I was a child. She moved into the house next door to us a few years before my father's death. Auntie Maria arrived one day in a small bakkie with only a few belongings – a bed, a two-seater sofa, sealed boxes. She didn't have a fridge and for a few months shared ours. Ma kept an entire shelf for Auntie Maria's perishables – long-life milk, eggs, Stork margarine, occasionally polony and cheese, which we eyed with drool dripping from our mouths. We watched the two men unload boxes and take them into Auntie Maria's house. They were gone within an hour. Auntie Maria remained behind, alone. Ma waited for what she called a respectable amount of time to pass before crossing our yard to the new neighbour, Mbuso and I trailed along.

We live in an old section of the township, a close-knit community where everyone knows everyone; new arrivals stand out like thorns. We learned that Auntie Maria had moved to the house next door after her husband's forgetfulness became too much to bear. He had forgotten small, insignificant things at first, but soon he couldn't remember how to tie his laces, would pause mid-sentence in the middle of a conversation before continuing on an unrelated thread, and once looked at Auntie Maria steadily and said, "Gogo, where have you been? We've been looking all over for you." That's when Auntie Maria had taken him to the mental hospital for assessments. A few weeks later he had almost burned down the kitchen after leaving a piece of paper on the hot stove, claiming his mother had asked him to start a fire to prepare the evening meal.

"I couldn't handle it, Margaret," Auntie Maria explained. She had taken him back to the hospital and left him there. She told Ma that their house became too big and empty once the children moved out. Her husband died shortly after; he did not know who Maria was. Ma, fighting back tears after listening to Auntie Maria, pointed at us and said we were now also her children. The two women had burst out laughing. Many years later, after my father's death and Ma's breakdown, Auntie Maria became our other mother.

* * *

Doctor Thusi arrives. Sizwe opens the gate and lets him in. After a polite exchange of customary greetings and passing words of comfort to the grieving mother, I lead the doctor to the room with Fikile's dead body. The hearse has not arrived.

He sits next to her, lowers the blanket covering her face, and stares with afflicted resignation, wounds raw. Doctor Thusi loved Fikile. Years ago when she and Thiza were separated, years before her cancer, Doctor Thusi had declared his intention – he wanted to take Fikile as a wife. My sister declined his advances. The doctor was wounded. He wrote Fikile a long letter, his writing precise and not resembling the medication scripts he scribbled daily for his patients. He wrote that he could not understand how she refused him when he was offering her so much more than the man who had fathered her two children, a man not worthy of a fine woman like her. *My heart will forever yearn for you*, the doctor ended the letter. And it did, long after Fikile went back to Thiza and fell pregnant with Bafana, and he, Doctor Thusi, married a nurse from the local hospital and built her the loveliest house in New Hope.

Doctor Thusi takes Fikile's limp hand, holds it to his chest. I look away. "Your sister was a beautiful soul. I'm sorry I couldn't save her," he says, choking on his tears. I want to tell the doctor he can't possibly blame himself for Fikile's death, that, if anything, he had given her the gift of a few more years with us. Instead, I pat his shoulder and leave him with his despair.

Dawn begins to break.

One by one, the children file out of Ma's bedroom wiping sleep from their eyes as they stumble to the fully occupied lounge. A hysterical Lesihle squeezes her slim frame in between her grandmother and Auntie Maria. Ma's voice is cool and controlled over Lesihle's fiery screams. Mvula cries, and Bafana looks at me with tears filling behind his eyelids.

The hearse arrives. We stand outside on the veranda watching it take Fikile's body away. We slowly walk back inside the house.

we do not have a history of
cancer in the family

Doctor Thusi found a lump in Fikile's left breast eight months after she gave birth to Bafana. My sister was thirty-one years old. I had gone over to Fikile's house as I often did in those days to drop off basic groceries and relieve her of baby duties. I also had my own good news to share, having finally taken the pregnancy test that morning after my period was a week late. I wanted her to be the first to know.

As I approached Fikile's kitchen, I was greeted by aromas of rosemary and lemon and spices. I found her sitting by the table surrounded by mounds of half-chopped vegetables. Fikile gestured for me to place the bags on the sink counter.

"What is it?" I asked, examining her face. Having cooked for Ma, Mbuso and I throughout her teens instead of loitering with friends, exchanging notes on boys and writing pop music lyrics in A4 college exercise books, Fikile loathed cooking. In the early years of their relationship, Thiza had complained about Fikile's lack of domesticity, the absence of rich meat stews and pap and Sunday's seven colours at the lunch table, and when it was clear that Fikile was not yielding to his pressure, he had told her jokingly that she shouldn't be surprised if he went elsewhere to be fed like a man should be. Fikile had snorted and said she would bet a cow that even if she cooked all day for him, he would still go out and poke his penis in other women's vaginas.

I looked around the kitchen that afternoon, at the cut meat pieces marinating by the fridge, the steam bread bubbling on the stove. This was a feast; my sister was not known for cooking up a storm randomly.

I took a seat next to her, alarmed. "Fikile, what happened?"

"Nothing, I'm just being a good wife cooking for her family. Is that a crime?" Fikile's voice was strained as if she had been crying. She coughed to break the phlegm. "I do cook sometimes, you know." A tight smile appeared on her face. "Your problem is that you're always suspicious. Relax, I'm fine."

I regarded my sister once more. She shook her head and continued grating the piece of carrot in her hand.

"Okay, sisi, if you say so. Where is everyone? Where is my *boy boy*?"

"The baby is sleeping. The others are out there in the streets; home is boring you see. My children are complaining that I make them do things – fetch this and that, make me tea, rub my feet – they don't like that. Lesihle is pissed off by the whole baby thing. She says I don't even talk to her except to tell her to do something. To retaliate, my children make themselves as scarce as possible."

"Must be hard for her, all the attention taken away from her by someone who can't even say Mama."

"Tough luck. We've all had to contend with younger siblings. You were the same with Mbuso."

"No, you lie. I loved that boy."

"Ask Ma, before Mbuso came it was you and dad. I was

sick with jealousy. Then he happened, and ruffled the order. Not that Dad loved you or me less, but Mbuso had him wrapped around his tiny finger. And him being a boy made Dad gooey with affection."

"I wish Baba was still alive," I said to Fikile who was mixing the grated carrot and cabbage. I stood and took out mayonnaise from the fridge and handed it to her. I was dying to tell my sister about the growing bundle in my stomach, but was determined to figure out what had triggered this uncharacteristic behaviour. I did not believe that it was nothing.

"Me too. Life would be different, good, I believe."

"Anyway, where is the man of this house?"

Fikile rolled her eyes. "Seriously?"

"Never mind. What can I help with, have you eaten, taken a bath at all today? How long have you been stewing in this kitchen in the name of good housekeeping?"

"Everything is under control." Fikile was silent for a moment, then burst out, "I have something to tell you."

"I knew it. What?"

"I saw Doctor Thusi this morning."

"Is the baby okay?"

"Yeah, Bafana is fine," she paused, started to chew on her lower lip. "It's me. Doctor Thusi found a lump, a sizable messy thing, right here," she said touching her left breast, the culprit breast, as if to reprimand it. "I went to see him because of a pain in my breast just below the nipple that refused to go away, even after taking countless painkillers."

"What?" I said out loud, unintentionally. "What?"

"A lump, here. Can't you see it looks funny?"

"A lump?"

"It's here, been here for some time, don't know how I missed it. But then, when was the last time I checked my breasts? When was the last time you checked yours?" Fikile lifted her shirt and bra, exposing her breast. She raised her left arm over her head in the way I'd seen illustrated in magazine articles and pamphlets on how to check your breasts for lumps and other unusual things. I couldn't remember the last time I touched mine that way.

"Is it serious?" I asked, touching the spot her index finger was pointing to.

"Here." Fikile took my hand and guided it to the area just beneath her full breast.

I only felt the softness and warmth of her skin. I shook my head, withdrew onto my seat, my hand trembling. "Is it cancer?"

"I don't know yet, have to get it tested. It's probably nothing. Breasts are lumpy anyway, and I've just had a baby, all sorts of things could be going on in there."

"When are you going?"

"Next week. Will you come with me?"

I nodded.

My face must have been plastered in terror because Fikile said, "Oh, gosh, Anele, wipe that look of death off your face. I'll be fine."

I remained glued to my seat watching my sister finish

34

preparing her feast. I'm certain she spoke to me, and I responded. I'm also certain we even laughed at something or someone or both. Yet, when I was driving home after she had dished up for the children, and packed some food for us in her matching Tupperware, I remembered nothing of our conversation. I arrived home and served Sizwe and Ma, then went into the bathroom, and for the longest time touched and squeezed my breasts until they become tender and painful. I heard Sizwe call my name and ask if I was okay in there.

* * *

Doctor Thusi had referred Fikile to a radiologist in town for a mammogram. Fikile and I drove to their offices. A few days later, Fikile received a call to come see Doctor Thusi to discuss the results of her tests. We did not talk about the tests during the short drive to the doctor's surgery in New Hope, though we both knew that a call from the doctor's office was never a good sign. Doctor Thusi gave away nothing as he cheerfully embraced and ushered us into his consulting room. His manner was still amiable as he poured a little too cold water into our glasses that gave me a momentary brain freeze, and marvelled at Bafana's growth (as if he couldn't wait to catch up with his siblings, the doctor said laughing), and as he asked about our mother's wellbeing. I forgot for a moment our business there.

"About your tests," Doctor Thusi said, jolting my mind back. He opened a drawer and pulled out several X-ray sheets, studying them intently as if seeing them for the first time. His jaw tightened for a second. "I'm afraid there is something in your breast, but we don't need to be alarmed."

Fikile and I hunched forward and watched the doctor point at the black-and-white film showing the web of veins and tissue, Fikile's breast. The mammogram had confirmed our fears, a lump the size of a large marble had lodged itself neatly under her nipple. Fikile needed a core needle biopsy, a procedure to remove a sample of breast tissue to test for cancer. He gave Fikile a business card of the surgeon who would assist her.

"We don't need to be alarmed," the doctor said again with measured concern, I thought. I turned to Fikile, seeking out her face, but she was already standing to take the envelope.

We left Doctor Thusi's office each engrossed in the chatter in our heads. Only when we were in the car, me behind the wheel, trying to suppress the threatening tears, the results of the mammogram in a large brown envelope on the back seat, did Fikile bring up the subject.

"I agree with Doctor Thusi, there is no need for alarm," she said, her voice full of conviction.

"We do not have a history of cancer in the family, on both sides, so it can't be cancer," I pointed out, the steering wheel clutched in my hands such that I had to take turns wiping my palms on my skirt.

"I know, right? And I don't smoke or drink, and I had my children at a good age." Fikile leaned back and closed her eyes. "That's why I think it's nothing."

We had spent the days before getting the results consuming every bit of literature we could lay our hands on regarding breast cancer and watching videos of survivors. We had filled our vocabulary with new words – stage I-IV, metastasis, tumour, benign, malignant, mastectomy, chemotherapy, radiology, breast prosthesis, remission; words that until then had existed in other worlds, not ours. We had concluded Fikile was not at risk.

But in the car my doubt set in. I stole a glance at Fikile on the passenger seat. At that moment, the afternoon sun's rays shone through, emanating a halo around her face. She looked like an angel from our childhood biblical stories who had descended on earth to protect us. The image lasted a split second. Many years later when Fikile's illness finally caught up with her, I went back to that moment, to me it was the day she died. Or rather the day I killed my sister.

We drove in silence for the rest of the way. I looked straight ahead with concentrated effort.

When I stopped at the gate at our house, Fikile said she didn't want to come inside. "I want to go home. Please don't say anything to Ma yet."

"Okay."

"It's nothing, you'll see," Fikile said again.

* * *

My sister and I never told Ma anything. When we were young – I must have been ten – Fikile started her periods. I noticed the rusty spot on her white denim shorts. We were in the kitchen; Fikile was bent over the sink rinsing pumpkin leaves for dinner and I was grinding peanuts to go with the pumpkin leaves. Ma had not returned home from work and Baba was on the road. My then four-year-old brother, Mbuso, was outside by the gate waiting for Ma as he often did.

"Go get your brother, he needs to take his bath before the water gets cold," Fikile snapped.

"Are you hurt, Fikile?" I asked, pointing at the spot.

"What do you mean?" Fikile responded without turning.

"You're bleeding at the back."

"What?" Fikile twisted her neck. "Where?"

"There, your bum."

Fikile rushed out of the kitchen. Her loud scream made me ditch the peanuts and dash over to see what was happening.

"Don't come in," Fikile yelled, locking the door.

I leaned against the door and started to cry, to myself at first, but the tears came flooding out, soaking my face and neck down to my T-shirt; I did not realise I was sobbing loudly.

"Stop, I'm not hurt," Fikile yelled from the other side of the door.

But I couldn't stop. I started to shake and couldn't breathe from hiccups. The door was yanked open and Fikile came out holding the soiled shorts and underwear in a tight ball under her arm.

"Anele, I told you I'm not hurt. I have a period. It happens

38

to girls once they reach a certain age, part of growing up."
She held me tightly with her free arm until my hiccups
subsided.

I followed Fikile outside to the laundry area, and watched
her soak the soiled clothing in soapy water with bleach.

"It will be over in a few days," she said.

I was scared. "I don't want a period," I said finally when
we were back in the kitchen to our respective tasks.

Fikile laughed. "You can't stop it. It's one of those things
that happen naturally to women. If we didn't have periods,
we would not be able to have babies, which means you and
I wouldn't be here. Listen, don't tell Ma about this, okay?"

"Okay, I won't."

"Promise?"

"Promise."

When I got my first period a couple of years later, I only
told Fikile.

* * *

Fikile's surgeon's name was Doctor Seme. We arrived early
and met her at the consulting room in the basement of the
hospital. She said she had heard a lot about Fikile from Doctor Thusi. Over good, strong coffee for me and sweet rooibos
tea for Fikile and herself, Doctor Seme took her time to
explain the biopsy to us. She showed us pictures of a giant
needle piercing through breast tissue and explained the
possible outcomes of the biopsy and what would happen
afterwards.

"I don't like what I see from the mammogram. Let us determine what we're dealing with first, then nip whatever is growing on your breast in the bud," she said. Fikile listened intently throughout. My lower body went numb. Fikile agreed to return for the procedure three days later.

The doctor performed the biopsy in less than an hour and sent the breast tissue for testing. We left the hospital with hope in our hearts.

A week later Fikile and I returned for the results.

Fikile had cancer alright. Doctor Seme said they would have to cut out the cancer-infested tumour, and might be able to save her breast. The lymph node closest to the tumour would also be removed to test if the cancer had spread. Radiation therapy would assist in eliminating cancer cells remaining in the breast tissue. "And hopefully that will be all that's needed to get your health in top form again."

The procedure, called a lumpectomy, was done in under an hour. I took Fikile home and spent the night with her and the children. Except for telling Thiza and Sizwe, we had not fully disclosed Fikile's condition to the family.

A few days later Doctor Seme called, and we found ourselves back in her office. I sat with my arms folded over my chest and fixed my eyes on the piece of paper in the doctor's hands. Doctor Seme did not offer us a drink. She had bad news, she began, slowly as if unsure of her words. Very bad news indeed.

"Not what I hoped for, not at all what I hoped for," she repeated.

The cancer had spread to the lymph nodes, and it appeared aggressive, attacking and mutating and destroying everything along its path. The breast and affected nodes would have to go. And then there would be chemo and radiation therapy and five years of hormone treatment to reduce the chances of the cancer returning, Doctor Seme said.

The word "mastectomy" danced in front of my eyes. Fikile didn't bat an eyelid, which was just as well because my downpour in Doctor Seme's office was enough for both of us. Instead, she sat up straight, looked at the doctor and said in the most serious tone, "When can we do the surgery?"

The doctor smiled. "Breast cancer is a war. You are already on your way to winning the battle with your positive spirit."

She scheduled the surgery to take place in two weeks.

I called a meeting of close family members to share the news about Fikile's cancer. Ma wept, asked why God had not given the cancer to her, and pleaded with him to spare Fikile's life to raise her children. Auntie Betty scolded Ma, said she was being dramatic and childish. Ma told Auntie Betty that she wouldn't understand, that only women who had given birth would understand her anguish. Auntie Betty rolled her eyes, took her tub of snuff and went outside. We heard her sneeze several times. Auntie Ntombi, the youngest of the three sisters, quoted impressive survival statistics. She mentioned friends of friends who walked around without breasts and were just as alive as women with both breasts. Thiza sat quietly throughout, and later got smashed; Sizwe had to pick him up from the local tavern and drive him home. Fikile took a pair of pantyhose and moulded it into a tight ball and, lifting it up, said laughing, "I've always wanted to have perky boobs."

No one laughed with her.

"Come on. People live through cancer, right? It's not a death sentence. I'll beat it," Fikile protested. "I will."

After Ma and my aunts had prayed for Fikile, long prayers I did not know they were capable of spewing from their mouths, and everyone had gone, I called Mbuso. I had not spoken to my brother in months, and had not seen him since that incident at his wedding earlier in the year, which had left a spectacular awkwardness between him and Fikile. Mbuso said he would come on the day of the operation, he asked me to keep his visit between us, he said he was not ready to face the rest of the family.

All through this, Fikile hadn't cried.

*   *   *

We congregated in the hospital waiting room on the day of Fikile's operation – me, Auntie Betty, Auntie Ntombi, Ma, Sizwe and Thiza – raising eyebrows and murmurs from other visitors and hospital staff as we tried unsuccessfully to keep our voices down. Ma read a verse and prayed every few minutes. We all joined at Amen. Doctor Thusi showed up. He spoke quietly to Fikile just before they wheeled her to theatre. He held her hand to his chest and cried. I had never seen him cry before.

42

Two days later as we were driving home after Fikile was discharged, I wanted to know what Doctor Thusi had said.

"He said it's not the end of the world, that I will live long enough to see Bafana attend university. Do you believe him?"

"You will live. You have to live."

"I know, I know. I must live. I'm not yet done with this world," Fikile said, and closed her eyes.

*   *   *

The operation to remove Fikile's breast went off without a hitch. I held her hand the whole time until we reached the theatre doors. Mbuso arrived shortly after Fikile was wheeled into theatre. I slipped off and met him in the parking lot. We sat inside his car and spoke about Fikile's diagnosis and everyone's wellbeing. Mbuso mumbled something about his wife, Mapule.

"I'm glad you came, Mbuso. Look, I don't want to meddle in your life or tell you what to do, but at some point, you must return home. Ma is a wreck, and we're all trying everything to manage the pain but it's tough. I can't bear to think of our lives without Fikile."

"She will be fine."

"We need you, Mbuso."

My brother negotiated with the night nurses to see Fikile after the visiting hours, after we had all left and gone home. And then he was gone.

After she was discharged, I went straight from work to

see her every evening. I helped her drain the blood and tissue fluid from the wound. After the tubes were removed, we sat on her bed stretching her arms to reduce the stiffness from the operation. Although Fikile was in pain, she did not once ask, "Why me?" or "What have I done to deserve this?"

Doctor Seme removed the bandages when ten days had passed. We watched as she peeled them off revealing scar tissue, a deep, brown line running from Fikile's left armpit through the middle of the chest. Her other breast, the healthy one, stood upright and defiant.

"Do I look hideous?" Fikile looked directly at me.

I sensed apprehension in her voice.

"You know what it reminds me of? Remember when Lesihle was two or three and learning to draw straight lines? Everything was a canvas for her, waiting for her lines."

Fikile threw her head back and laughed. We started referring to her breast as Lesihle's line. A month later, she called one of the companies listed in a brochure she had picked up at the hospital and made an appointment to fit a breast prosthetic and mastectomy bra. Fikile was clear that she would not reconstruct her breast yet, she said her scars would serve as a reminder of what she'd been through. I drove with her to the fittings.

The shop, located in a small shopping centre, looked like any lingerie shop with its displays of mannequins in racy allures of reds and black mesh and lace underwear. We were welcomed by the owner who proceeded to take Fikile's measurements, chatting to her like it was a normal bra fitting, as if Fikile did not have a thin line where her left breast once was. I sat on the couch drinking cold bubbly with a cherry dancing at the bottom of my glass and browsing through a women's health magazine. Occasionally I lifted my eyes to scrutinise Fikile's bra parade, screaming "Yes, that's the one!" or frowning in disapproval. Fikile did not leave the shop with a handful of bras and a white nightdress with black lace trims, she left a complete woman.

On our way home I broke the news of my pregnancy. My sister said it was the best news ever, a sign of new life and longevity for the family. She said she knew she would beat cancer. She directed me to a lodge outside town, a place I had never been to nor had known existed. She said it was her favourite place in the world. We ordered rump steak and grilled potatoes and glazed pumpkin; we ate until our tummies threatened to burst.

The next morning Fikile met with her oncologist.

* * *

We had not anticipated the fatigue of chemotherapy. Once every two weeks for twenty-four weeks, Thiza, once, and I drove Fikile to treatments at her oncologist's office. We all drove with Fikile on the first day of her chemotherapy treatment, and crammed the small waiting room, which resulted in Fikile forbidding visitations by more than one person at a time. I sat with her as the nurse drew her blood for testing, and held her hand as an IV was inserted into her right arm, allowing the drugs to drip into the bloodstream. We stayed in the hospital for five hours. Fikile would repeat this procedure many times. After each treatment Fikile came back as if a small part of her was taken away; she appeared a little less complete. She complained of constant waves of nausea and vomit that threatened to pull her guts out, mouth sores, and hot flushes that left sweat marks on her bed. And pain, she was overcome by pain, in her back, her legs, her head. She lost her sense of taste. Fikile slept for hours, sometimes days at a time. She stopped going to work fulltime, leaving her assistant to manage the early childhood development centre, a three-roomed structure she had opened adjacent to the church a couple of years before her diagnosis.

"I will not bow down to this disease. I have a life to live, kids to raise, bills to pay," Fikile said each time after recovering from the chemo session, full of optimism, ready to resume her life. "I can't die. This cancer must be defeated. No, this cancer will be defeated."

Fikile also refused to move in with us during her treatment, even after Ma threatened her in our dead father's name. My sister was defiant, said she was capable of looking after herself and her family. But she couldn't. Lesihle called, sometimes in tears, to alert us to another dizzy spell that left her mother crawling on the kitchen floor. So, for a couple of days after each session, Ma packed up her life and deposited herself at Fikile's doorstep and took over the household.

By the end of her third chemo session, a wedge of hair

had fallen off in the middle of Fikile's head, leaving a bald dry patch that even thick braids could not conceal. Fikile asked Sizwe to shave off the rest. When he was done, he gave Fikile a mirror. I stood watching her, my belly knotted.

Fikile gasped when she saw herself, then a broad smile spread across her face. I exhaled.

"I'm too beautiful for New Hope, I should have been a superstar."

"You are a superstar."

"Maybe. All I need is red lipstick and some blush, don't you think?" She started wearing lipstick every day after that.

Radiation therapy followed. Fikile said those few weeks were like living under earth. Only after she completed her radiation therapy did she have a good cry. She couldn't stop, as if every scrap of tension was breaking loose from her body. And with that, she believed, the cancer was too. We slaughtered two goats and brewed sorghum beer to thank our ancestors and the doctors and God, and everyone who prayed for Fikile's recovery.

the burial business is
big in new hope

An unexpected calm descends upon our house as we gather in the family room. Although nobody says it, we are all thinking it: Fikile is finally resting. The children, in their animal print and Afro-rocking princess inspired pyjamas, watch the morning's programmes on a national television channel on low volume, and dip buttered bread into sweet milky tea. Lesihle has taken to policing Bafana and Mvula, she tells them to keep their voices low, that there is death in the family. Mvula wants to know who has died, and why, and if that person has gone to heaven like her friend from school. She was devastated when that happened. Although she knew that heaven was a good place, where children sang "Jesus Loves Me" songs all day, she worried that soon it would be her turn to go and she was not ready yet. She refused to leave the house for days, afraid a big, bad car would knock her down just as it did her friend.

"Don't be stupid, Mvula," Lesihle hisses. "The hearse came to take my mother's body away."

"What is a hearse?"

"A car that takes dead people away."

"To where, heaven?"

"No, to the mortuary until their relatives collect their bodies to bury. The hearse came just now to take my mother."

"Mama Fikile?"

"Yes. Gosh, you're slow."

"What happens if the people do not have families to bury them?"

"Everyone has a family to bury them," Lesihle answers.

"Well, what if one person does not?"

Lesihle stares at her cousin with a mixture of annoyance and contemplation. After a couple of minutes, she responds with an air of victory, "The government will bury that person. Now stop asking me questions and keep quiet."

Bafana looks pensively at his sister as if processing her words, leans over to Mvula, and speaks in a muted tone, only meant for his cousin's ears. "My mother is dead. We will never see her again."

"Oh, I forgot," Mvula says, turning to her tea, swallowing the rest of the mushy mix that has collected at the bottom of the cup.

In the kitchen, Ma randomly calls out names of people that still need to be notified – distant relatives whose names I don't recognise, friends, the church members, parents of the children who attended Fikile's crèche, the entire section of our location, Ma's friends. She is worried she has left out important names, but I tell her people will find out on their own, they always do. Ma's face is laced with premature wrinkles and there are dark circles under her eyes, the havoc of alcohol abuse blatantly showing each time she is under strain.

"I should have called Reverend Madida to deliver a prayer soon after Fikile returned from the hospital," she laments.

"You didn't know she would die."

"I know, my child. It's just that Reverend Madida was fond of your sister. The whole congregation – they were all so fond of her. They will be devastated."

We agree with Ma to bury Fikile on Saturday, early before the sun is high. I debate whether to wait for Thiza or go to the funeral home to sort out the details of Fikile's funeral on my own. I am wary of causing an even deeper rift between us, but we also can't wait for him forever, we need to confirm Fikile's funeral date and time or forget a Saturday morning burial. As it is, we will be lucky to be on the waiting list. The burial business is big in New Hope.

After the cancer returned, Fikile had insisted on being buried within three days of her death. She said she wanted the ordeal over and done with, no prolonged fervour of mourning. Ma would not hear of it.

"You want people to think we're trying to get rid of you? You want people to think we're embarrassed by your death?" Ma protested.

"I don't care about people, Ma. Whoever needs to see me off will make an effort to come," Fikile asserted. "You keep me frozen for a long time, I will cause an uproar. I swear, Ma, chairs will fly. The earth will move, crack in all places, thunderbolts like you've never seen in your life before."

"Fikile, stop it, we hear you," I said, suppressing a laugh.

"You think this is a joke?" Ma passed a solid look from Fikile to me. "You think death is funny?"

"No, Ma, death is not funny, Fikile is telling us what she

wants, surely we must honour her wishes?" I said. "She doesn't want her body to rot at the mortuary. Do you trust their refrigerators? Do you think they work properly?"

"Yes, Ma, let me speak now," Fikile said. "I haven't had much of a say in many things in this life, allow me at least to plan my funeral. Better yet, why not get cremated? You know, white people are so clever, they don't spend money on absurd things like coffins, things that rot anyway."

"I don't appreciate the way you two are talking, it's hurtful. Fikile, take back everything you've said." Ma was on the verge of crying; the corner of her mouth began to quiver. She pushed her reading glasses up and turned her gaze away from us. I had not seen her shake like that since the time she was admitted at a government detoxification facility.

"Ma, you know I'm dying. Look at me." Fikile's tone was serious. She gestured with her hands at her wasted body. "This is not a body of someone full of health, I'm sick. My body is at war with itself and there is no medication to help me. No cure. There is no point for us to teeter around this issue anymore. We're all adults here and we must be practical and talk about what will happen after I'm dead – the funeral, my children." Fikile was always firm with Ma, the only person who could be.

"Fikile, please. You're taking this too far," I interjected.

"Am I? Is the cancer not in my lungs and liver and God knows where else in my body? Is it not? Look, we may not have another chance to talk. I know Thiza took out life policies for me and is paying good money for them; he will be filthy rich after I die. Anele, I want you to tell him you know about the money. I want you to tell him that my children should not go hungry or not get a good education because of his greed. Promise me."

Ma eyed her briefly, hurt and defeated, exhaled sharply and started to make her way out of the room.

"Mama, don't go. Fine, I take back the cremation and the three days, but anything more than a week I will not tolerate. And I'm serious about the policies."

I nodded, though Fikile knew very well she was asking the impossible, Thiza parting with money? It would never happen. I was aware of the policies Fikile was referring to, life insurance and funeral covers Thiza had taken to cover her – forty thousand here, one hundred and fifty thousand there. It all added up to something significant. Shortly after Fikile completed her chemo and radiation treatments the first time, she had shown me the documents.

"Look here, funeral covers, life covers, all kinds, and I'm in all of them. Bastard is planning to cash up when I die."

"You're being dramatic. You are sick, yes, but you will not die. What I want to know is, where does he get the money to pay for this? How much money is he making from renting his shops, surely it can't be that much?"

"My darling husband pays for everything with his dick, don't you know that?"

"The same one that got you into trouble in the first place."

"Same dick, what can I say. It's like Thiza is saying hurry up and die so I can live."

Within a few months the conversation was different, Fikile was dying and we couldn't pretend otherwise. I remembered that moment in Doctor Seme's office when she said it wasn't looking good, not good at all. Fikile had lost nearly half of her body weight, Bafana struggled the most with the changes in his mom. Once Fikile had spent a few weeks at the hospital after she came down with an infection. When Bafana saw her, he cried and called her "ghost". Lesihle held his hand and said, "It's not a ghost, it's Mama."

*　*　*

As the eldest child, Fikile was always responsible for the logistics of our family events. Together with my aunts, she schemed for days concocting mouth-watering menus, organising stretch tents and Tiffany chairs and tables, picking out the right type of animal to sacrifice. My job was limited to contributing a few frozen chicken packs, ten kilograms of rice and flour, and cooking oil, showing up on the eve of the event to assist with peeling vegetables, and offering my car for general use if I was feeling charitable – but with a list of terms and conditions.

But Fikile is gone now.

Thiza's phone is still off. I leave a message this time: it's urgent, call me. I decide to arrange my sister's funeral without my brother-in-law's input.

From the house I drive to the funeral home, a lone, single-storey lime building lying proud in the middle of a corner stand, massive and impressive. The main gate, a wrought iron structure with a decorative sculpture of an elephant, trunk broken in the middle, stands wide and open for business. Hearses, big and small, white like purity with golden crosses embossed on their bonnets, are parked in a neat line under the shaded parking. By the weekend the cars will stream out of the funeral home to various destinations across the location to collect the dead and deliver them to the township's two cemeteries. A large white-letter sign with the inscription *Vilakazi Funeral Undertakers: We Are With You At The Time Of Need* sits perched high up on the outside wall of the entrance.

I park my car in the visitors' parking and pause to catch my breath and wipe the sweat forming on my brow. Fikile's funeral policy is tucked inside my handbag.

We took the burial plans at the same time, years before Fikile's diagnosis. It was the year of new beginnings for us. I had graduated a year before with a Bachelor of Accounting Sciences in Financial Management from UNISA, and had a new government job as an accountant. It was a junior position with low pay, but it came with paid leave, pension and medical aid, things I had not had access to before. Fikile was armed with a national diploma in Early Childhood Development and a dream to start her own crèche. We were both high with knowledge and promise of financial independence.

The air is cool and dry inside the funeral parlour. My mind wanders to the sound of the refrigerators humming at the back stuffed with dead bodies: I see Fikile's body, cold but not yet stiff with ice, wrapped in the faded floral sheet it came in.

"Can I help you?" It is the voice of a young woman seated at the desk closest to the door. She is wearing a black T-shirt with the parlour's logo of a white flying dove above her left breast. She has a warm, trained smile. I move towards her.

"I'm Anele Mabuza. My sister's body was brought here this morning." From my handbag I take out the crumpled manila envelope with Fikile's funeral cover and hand it over to her.

The young woman introduces herself as Nina. She only has a few questions for me – time of Fikile's passing, cause of death. She is respectful throughout, does not pry for details about Fikile's death and spares me compassionate talk.

"Excuse me." She stands and walks over to one of the steel cabinets lining the wall, and pulls out a small folder. "Everything is in order," Nina says after paging through Fikile's file. "Here, this is what you will be getting from the Essential Funeral Plan." She shows me a picture of the coffin my sister will be buried in, a solid wood casket, with simple gold trimmings and plain white silk interior, what Fikile had chosen for herself. The package includes a small blue-and-white tent, a set of twenty-five plastic chairs, forty bottles of water, a hundred printed funeral programmes, and grocery money to help on the day. She asks me if we would like to brand the water bottles with Fikile's photo or name or something. I tell her no.

"Would you like to see the actual coffin?"

"No, it's not necessary."

"Who will come to dress your sister?"

"What?"

"Dress your sister on Friday," she repeats. "Someone must come and wash and dress your sister before taking her home."

I have not thought of this. "My aunts," I say. "My aunts will."

"Please tell them to arrive early, otherwise it gets busy in the afternoon."

I know what she means. Scores of bereaved families will descend on the funeral home to fetch their departed in preparation for the next day's burial. Rows of cars with their hazards on, driving slowly, with dignity, inconsolable families inside, heads down, following the hearses. This time, we will be part of the procession.

I thank the young lady and leave.

* * *

I can tell by the booming voice coming from the house that Auntie Betty has arrived. I can't contain my relief and fleetingly forget the heaviness of the two grocery bags in my hands. My aunt will know what to do.

Ma and Auntie Betty have removed the mattress on which Fikile died and placed it in the garage, and pushed the furniture in the lounge against the walls such that there is space to accommodate additional chairs. I'm not surprised that at their age, with a handful of children and grandchildren, and a dead husband in between, they have the strength to manoeuvre large pieces of furniture with only tiny beads of sweat showing on their foreheads. I recall as a child how Auntie Betty, assisted by Ma, slaughtered a Boer goat to prepare for a family ceremony marking the end of Ma's mourning period. The sun was going down and the men were at the back of the house feasting on traditional beer and biltong someone had brought along. Auntie Betty became agitated. She and Ma cornered the animal, held its feet together and with a single, precise movement, Auntie Betty slit its throat. The goat jerked once, and died with a whimper. I was sent to fetch a bowl, which Ma placed under the goat's bleeding neck. I secretly dipped my finger in the blood and was surprised by its warmth. Auntie Ntombi in her freshly manicured nails, and long black pants and pink silk shirt stood by the kitchen door the entire time, watching and wincing and making funny noises and teasing them about how farm life would always be part of them. Ma and Auntie Betty ignored her. They proceeded to skin the goat, hanging the skin to dry, cutting off the head, carefully separating the bile, and cleaning the offal and organs and the carcass. By the time someone at the back shouted, "Imbuzi," Ma and Auntie Betty were preparing the fire to boil the tripe.

"What did you get, a casket?" Ma asks, her voice full of expectations. "I was telling your aunt about the coffin in which my friend Ma Mlambo's child was buried, like a castle. I'm convinced the young man is going straight to heaven and he never even set foot in church."

I drop the groceries on the floor and pull out the picture of Fikile's coffin from my bag.

"It is fine," she says with a hint of disappointment. Not quite the palace of a casket she was expecting. She passes the brochure to Auntie Betty who says it's perfect. I smile at my aunt. Ma's outrageous demands for finer things in life were a wonder to us. She has not worked for more than twenty years, and has gone through life living on hand-outs and people's mercies. Yet this did not alter the perception of what she thinks she deserves, her family deserves.

"I suspect our mother was a queen in her previous life," Fikile once joked.

* * *

Mbuso, the prodigal son, is calling. I walk out of the room before Ma or Auntie Betty's prying eyes can turn my way, before they know it's him on the line. It's too soon to mention his name and evoke emotions, open unhealed wounds. I can imagine how coming home after such a long time must be nerve-racking for Mbuso, like a *Khumbul'-Ekhaya* episode.

"In today's episode of *Khumbul'Ekhaya,* we bring you Mbuso Mabuza, who is returning home after many years of absence." Camera zooms to a nervous-looking but determined Mbuso, in a crisp pink shirt and khaki cargo pants, trendy brown loafers. Ma runs out of the house into Mbuso's hesitant arms. "Why, my child, why have you forsaken us?" She wails. Mbuso glances at the camera, aware of the attention, attempts a response, but when none manifests in his mouth, tightens his arms around his mother. The end.

Except for the time Mbuso came to see Fikile at the hospital during her mastectomy and a few follow-up calls afterwards, Mbuso exists in photographs: Mbuso in a khaki shirt and shorts at a school outing at a game reserve; on his tenth birthday, blowing out a candle on his homemade chocolate cake; in torn jeans and a white T-shirt, shoes visibly bigger than his feet – Thiza's old shoes – flashing a peace sign. Occasionally Mvula asks about the young boy in a grey tracksuit, holding a tattered backpack and staring mischievously at the camera. Mbuso exists in things around the house: the old boombox that he played until Ma screamed at him to turn it off, rusting medals, the fossil BMX bike with its loose chain in the garage that Ma refuses to throw away. But mostly my brother exists in our memories.

"Bhuti, where are you?" From the kitchen window I notice Lesihle sitting on the boulders near the outdoor washing sink. Fikile's rocks.

It is behind these rocks that Fikile, later joined by me, snuck ice-cold ciders, or sometimes, when there wasn't enough money for ciders, cheap, boxed, dry white wine. The alcohol burnt our mouths and eyes, leaving us with wobbly knees, speaking slurred words to imaginary friends, nursing splitting headaches and hangovers that lasted for days, and occasionally burning dinners so that young Mbuso had to go to bed fed only on bread and tea. But Ma was too drunk to notice. Some years later, when it was Mbuso's turn to experiment with alcohol, he did not go behind the boulders; he brought home ingudu and gulped it in front of Ma. He was fifteen, and had started bunking school. Ma went inside her bedroom and cried.

"What is her problem? Is she upset because I won't share my beer with her? Has she ever given you a sip of hers?" Mbuso laughed. I scolded him and took the bottle from him. Mbuso continued to laugh, an evil laugh so mean and raw it left my skin tingling with fear. Later that evening I found him passed out on his bedroom floor, next to him a half-smoked joint. Panicked, I called Fikile; we were losing our younger brother.

"I'll be there soon," Mbuso says now on the other end of the line.

"Good. Mbuso?"

"Yes?"

"I'm glad you're coming."

"How is Ma?"

"Okay under the circumstances. Fikile's illness complete-ly sobered her up, Fikile's illness has sobered all of us. Well, except maybe for your brother-in-law. He hasn't shown his face, I don't know if he's battling with the loss or if he is being a prick, hard to say with Thiza."

"I won't be long now, let's deal with Thiza when I get there."

"Ma will be happy to see you. She still cries for you, after all these years. There are days when she wakes up only wanting to talk about you."

There is silence as if the line has gone dead.

"Mbuso?"

"I'm here."

I realise my mistake. "We will see you when you get here. Drive safely." I hang up before my brother changes his mind, turns around and returns to his beautiful family and white double-storey house in a gated community, a life far from his past. Only when I get off the phone I realise my second mistake: I have not asked Mbuso if he is bringing his wife. I wonder now if they have children, nephews and nieces, little Mabuzas. Mbuso has kept his private life away from us.

I sneak into Fikile's room to collect clean linen to prepare the outside room for Mbuso and his wife and maybe children. Fikile's house in the other section of the township is the place of formal bereavement from where the funeral proceedings will be conducted. But there will be too many of us to fit in Fikile's house. I open the thick lock of the outside room and let myself inside. Dust and stale air wafts off, triggering a coughing spree. I move quickly to open the only window and unhook the curtains and take them down, red with dust. I can't recall when last someone cleaned this room; Fikile's condition single-handedly managed to re-order our lives, draw up new agendas for us. I remove the beige sheet and the denim duvet cover Mbuso bought with his first pay cheque as a student tutor during his first year at university. I run the feather duster over the giant wall posters of 2Pac with his signature bandana and charm, framed school certificates, a few trophies from the debate club, from before Mbuso withdrew his membership in grade ten to the horror of his English class teacher. By that time, getting a word out of Mbuso was like squeezing water out of a cactus.

I sweep and mop the floor and when I'm satisfied with my efforts, I lie down on the freshly made bed, shut my eyes, and feel for a moment the burden of grief lift off and drift away.

* * *

I am awakened by Thiza's call. It takes a moment to establish my surroundings, to register the numbness in my heart.

"Thiza, where are you? Did you get my message about Fikile?"

"Yes, I did." Thiza's voice is muffled, as if coming from a hole a thousand kilometres below ground. "I'm trying to make sense of everything that has happened. I need time."

"Time for what? You do realise that people here are waiting for you? Your children are asking for you. Ma is getting restless, wanting us to call you every five minutes." I lower my voice, and speak with obligatory calm, "I understand you're dealing with the loss your way, but I'm asking you to be thoughtful towards others."

I hang up not knowing what Thiza needs time for. His wife is dead and he should be here planning her burial. I collect the dirty linen and join the women in the lounge. Auntie Maria has returned, now fully dressed, from next door.

"Where is the children's father?" Auntie Maria asks as

65

soon as I walk in. "Your aunt tells me he is yet to come pay his respects to his wife."

"He is on his way," I respond.

Ma sighs, says, "Thanks be to God."

Auntie Betty clicks her tongue, folds her arm.

Auntie Maria's face is heavy with curiosity. "Oh? So it could be true?"

We are silent for a moment.

"What?" Ma asks.

"Everyone is talking about it."

"What, Maria?" Ma asks again with suppressed irritation.

"That Thiza has moved in with the widow of Cele's eldest son, his name is not coming to me now, the one who worked at Home Affairs. He died in that horrible car accident by the bridge some years back. A good young man. You know the widow, Margaret. Nolwazi, that's her name."

Ma shakes her head.

"A tragic and sad time in our community. It didn't end well at all for the poor child; her husband's family made her life miserable. They said she killed him for insurance. Me, I didn't believe them. They took everything he left for her and their children. Everything. Anele, you must know them?" Auntie Maria turns to me for affirmation.

"I do."

"But God is great. That child refused to let her spirit be broken, she went after them like fire. I hear she hired a good lawyer, a woman, who helped her get the two cars, house and all the furniture back. Oh, she is comfortable now. Very

66

comfortable. I hear Thiza can be seen driving at high speed in one of her cars."

"You know people always have something to say, Maria," Auntie Betty says.

"People are talking, Betty." Auntie Maria leans back onto the sofa, arms tightly folded across her chest as if suddenly distancing herself from the rumour, then adds: "Are they lying though? I don't know. But I do know that the children's father is not here, and is not home either because Sizwe went looking for him. Don't hear me wrong, I'm not saying anything; I'm only pointing out the obvious."

"Ewu, Maria." It is not often that Auntie Betty runs out of words.

I focus my gaze on Ma who remains stoic as if Maria's unloading of the township gossip is not for her benefit. I struggle to read how much she is absorbing, how much grazes her ears like wind. She does not utter a word, her eyes are closed, she appears to be drifting in and out of grey sleep. Sizwe and I know the rumour, in fact everyone but Ma knows about Thiza and his other wife, Nolwazi.

like the first time

For four years, Fikile lived cancer-free. We celebrated Bafana's first birthday, welcomed baby Mvula, delightful with a
head of jet black curly hair and piercing dark eyes, went
shopping for pastel-coloured crop bras for Lesihle, bought
Khanya's high school uniform and textbooks, and watched
him elected head boy of his class. Fikile continued to take
her hormone treatment and checked in every six months.
Longevity and happiness were on our side. Then one day,
after a routine check, her oncologist called and asked her
to come back for a PET scan. They found something in the
scan, small clusters of cancer cells on her lungs and lymph
nodes and liver.

Fikile went to meet Doctor Seme. Alone. Later when she
was narrating her visit – at our home, in her old bedroom,
the bedroom she would later occupy and breathe her final
breath in – I had screamed at her, called her inconsiderate.
How could she?

My sister looked at me, and with a straight face said,
"Don't you see, this is my battle. You've done your part.
Now I must walk the rest of the road alone. Please try to
understand."

Doctor Seme said Fikile's cancer was no longer curable,
that it was all through her bloodstream. She said the best they
could do was prolong her life by cutting out the problematic

part of the lung and liver, and trying to burn the cancer with chemo and radiation therapy again. The doctor was sorry, so very sorry. She said there was no pattern with cancer.

"So, it will be like the first time?" I asked when I had dialled down my outrage to practical levels.

"No, it won't be like the first time," Fikile said, her voice breaking. It was only then that she started to show her vulnerability, that she started to appear scared. "I'm dying, for real this time. No one can save me."

We were foolish to believe the cancer would not fight back, stronger. Fikile was right, the battle was nothing like the first time. Within a few months, Fikile's lungs and liver became a haven for cancer cells. Week after week, Fikile was turned away from receiving treatment, her white cells were staging a protest. The cancer continued to eat away at her. The oncologist looked at the results and shook her head each time. There was nothing anyone could do.

We lay in the darkening room for a while without speaking. Images of Fikile, skeletal and bald, flashed in my mind. My sister had started to shed a few kilograms – muscle wasting away like a tree branch attacked by termites – but up until our chat, it hadn't crossed my mind that she might never gain it back.

Finally, Fikile leaned over and whispered, "Say something, please."

"I'm sorry," I said, lips trembling.

I rose from the bed. Blood rushed to my head, leaving me

faint. I sat back down to steady myself, breathed deeply, and stood up again. Everything was a blur – the light that shone inside the room a few minutes ago, illuminating and dreamlike, was replaced by shadows and death.

"Anele," Fikile called out, her voice thick with tears.

In the kitchen I stood by the sink for balance. Queasiness began to form in my gut, rising like hot vomit until it was arrested at the tip of my throat. I had experienced the same feeling when I had heard my sister, eighteen years old and concealing her pregnancy in layers of clothing, sob behind the closed door of her room, asking God to give her strength to let her child live. And when Mbuso declared how much he hated all of us, and how he couldn't wait to leave the dump of a home, never to return. Even though he was only fifteen years old at the time, full of hormones and rage, I believed him.

I opened one of the cabinets and took out a glass, filled it with water. I finished it in one gulp, refilled the glass, and drank it all up again. The nausea did not subside.

Fikile found me bent over in the garden.

"I'm sorry, Anele," she said patting my back.

"It's not fair you have to go through this again."

"I know, I know."

Fikile let me pour my guts out before leading us back inside.

"Promise you will look after my children."

"You will live."

"Promise me."

"Fikile, you know I won't allow anything to happen to your children."

"I think we should take the children to the coast, it's been a while since we had a family vacation. Bafana has been asking about the sea lately, he is fascinated by sharks and mermaids and ships. The ocean will be good for everyone."

It was our last holiday.

Soon after we returned, Fikile's energy started to seep out of her like a dripping tap. She stopped working again, stopped going to church. She abandoned her duty of seeing the children off to school, the last remaining duty she had appointed herself to do. She had insisted on making their school lunches, walking them to the gate, and pressing their developing, Vaseline-laden bodies to her diminishing frame. In the end, Fikile couldn't rise from the bed without help, and all she could muster by herself was a half-formed hug shared among the three children. She called it mommy's group hug. My aunts took turns visiting our house. They came with scones and frozen chicken pieces and toothpaste, practical items we were always running out of. Their presence did not only bring laughter and gossip, it renewed Ma's faith that her daughter would survive. Uncle Majaha called once a week and spoke to Fikile. I remember these calls being the happiest moments for my sister, her strength seemed to return at once as she cuddled the phone and giggled and promised our uncle that she wasn't going anywhere soon.

Then, two days before she died, her body broke into chills and then a fever.

being mbuso

A big white German SUV, the kind popular with the newly rich, quietly pulls inside our yard, parks under the fever tree a couple of metres from the gate. A few minutes pass before the car's occupant steps out. From where I'm seated, I watch through the lace curtain the lone figure that is my brother as he stretches and straightens his clothes. I watch him look out at the empty street – left, right, then to the house in front of him – his mind working furiously attempting to reconstruct the life he was once part of. I, too, begin to search my memory for him: a young Mbuso, age four, waiting by the gate for our father who always comes home with a surprise – sour worm sweets that left a bitter taste in our mouths forcing us to suck our cheeks involuntary, pieces of burnt sugar cane collected along his travels, a red toy race car for Mbuso, a cassette for Fikile, and a floor puzzle for me – until one day our father does not appear at the gate. Mbuso at six, the sun kissing his bare skin while he kicks a ball – homemade with rolled up plastic bags, rags, torn stockings, shreds of clothing, and strings – on the small patch of land opposite our house, until a string comes undone, Mbuso stops, picks it up, ties it firmly around the ball, and holds it up in triumph. Ten-year-old Mbuso coming home to change from his bloodied school uniform after a fight with one of the boys who made a joke about Ma.

Mbuso at fifteen, laughing cruelly, running away from Ma after she discovers he is stealing from her.

"Mbuso is here," I announce.

"Thank you, God, my son has arrived home safely," Ma says, flicking her eyes open.

"How long has it been since we last saw him?" Auntie Maria asks the question everyone asks whenever Mbuso's name is mentioned in a conversation; it is a surprise to all of us that Mbuso has managed to stay away from home for as long as he has. "I don't understand how one ups and leaves his family and does not return. The boy just went."

"The mention of Mbuso's name makes my blood boil," Auntie Betty says. "I never knew it was possible to be disrespected by a child this way, and for so long. This boy treats us like we are nothing to him."

"Auntie, please, calm down."

"Hhayi bo, Anele, don't tell me to calm down. Your brother has a lot to answer for." Auntie Betty frowns at me. "You want us to pretend that his actions have not hurt and embarrassed us? I won't. You know your aunt is not one to play the game of pretence."

"I ask that we bury first, hold court later."

"Don't you worry about that, we will bury Fikile. Then it will be Mbuso's turn to face the music, tell us where he gets the bravery to disappear on us, and the audacity to take a wife without involving us. Where have you ever heard such a thing?"

"But we were there," I say between my teeth.

"We were there! We were there! Please," Auntie Betty comments without skipping a beat. "If I were you, I wouldn't even mention that out loud, the whole thing was an embarrassment."

"Anele is right, we must give the boy a break," Ma says. "I'm happy he is here to lay his sister in her final place." Her voice is that of someone who has made peace with it all. It is as if she wants to say: Why bother with the blame game? The son's loathing of the mother, was it not her doing anyway? Did she not create the wrath?

"Lower your voices, he is coming up."

"Who is he with?" Auntie Betty asks.

"Alone."

"Alone? Where is the wife? You see, Margaret, this boy is still playing games with us. Why did he leave his wife behind? Is she not supposed to be here to help out with all the work around here? These modern boys are a problem."

"I don't know, maybe she will come later. She is a doctor, and this is a busy period for them, you know, with the carnage on our roads and people acting silly."

Even as I watch my brother standing under the tree and looking displaced, burdened, I feel a great sense of relief; the lost time between us is reduced to a week, a day, an hour, as if Mbuso has returned from a short holiday. It is a funny feeling, something warm moves within me, my body feels light. I look up because my eyes are clouding.

Cell phone in one hand, Mbuso takes a few uncertain steps towards the house of his childhood, his home. At that moment, I rush outside and fling my body into his waiting strong arms. I struggle to control the tears, tears and smiles; my brother is here.

"Fikile," Mbuso starts. "I'm sorry. I'm so sorry."

"I'm glad you came," I say over and over.

Mbuso holds on to me. We stand in the middle of the yard, clutching each other.

"Look at you," I say taking a step back, staring him up and down. "You've filled up since I last saw you, marriage agrees with you." Mbuso's tall, once lean frame has become soft with money. I poke at his protruding belly, round and taut, like that of a malnourished child. My brother takes after Ma: fair complexion as if there is white blood in the family, narrow nose, thick eyebrows that almost touch at the centre. Fikile and I are our father's children. We inherited his brown, moon-shaped face with stubborn broad noses. People said our eyes seem to twinkle with a million little stars. Ma gave all of us her height and good figure. "What took you so long to get here? I thought you were around the corner when we spoke."

Mbuso mumbles an excuse about long tollgate queues, speed traps, and roadblocks. Later he confesses that he stopped at a petrol station along the highway, forty-five minutes away, for almost an hour, too paralysed to proceed.

"I'm glad you didn't change your mind."

"I couldn't stay gone forever," he says.

"Come, they've been waiting for you."

"Who else is here with Ma?"

"Auntie Betty and Maria."

"Of course Auntie Betty is here." Mbuso removes his glasses and rubs his eyes violently, a habit developed as a child when he was nervous or angry or being Mbuso; the reason Ma believed he ended up needing glasses later.

"You'll be fine. They are looking forward to seeing you. Come, before the neighbours start arriving. Everyone has heard by now." I link my arm with his, lead him to the house.

The excitement and admiration of boy-turned-man in front of my mother and aunts is evident in their wide eyes. Grief is momentarily forgotten. No one speaks. Seven years is a long time.

Mbuso crouches in front of Auntie Betty who is closest to the door. "Mama."

"My son!" Auntie Betty grabs him and buries his face in her large bosoms. "My brother-in-law must be happy in the heavens seeing his son back where he belongs. Don't you ever leave us again, you hear me? We are your family. We are your blood and nothing will change that."

Mbuso nods emphatically, gasping for air.

"Do you remember who I am?" Auntie Maria enquires playfully. She takes both his hands, squeezes them together.

"Auntie, how can I forget someone who raised me?" Mbuso moves to hug her.

Finally he turns to Ma, who is sobbing uncontrollably.

Last time she saw Mbuso, he was still a teenager, home for his first, year-end university holidays. He was already a stranger then, preferring the company of his thick books and cell phone. We didn't know how to relate to him, he barely spoke to us. One evening, filled with alcohol-induced bravado, Ma barged into his room and screamed at him to leave her house if he wasn't happy with our company. She said he was making everybody around him miserable.

"Voetsek, hamba! We've had enough of your moping."

I tried to intervene though inwardly I was happy; we had suffered enough abuse in the few days Mbuso was home. Mbuso packed his bag and went to Fikile's house. The following morning he woke up early and left – not even Fikile could persuade him to stay until the university reopened. He did not visit home throughout his second year, said he had found a good-paying job not far from the university. He called us on Christmas Day and New Year. The following year was no different, and the years after that.

"Ma." Mbuso kneels next to Ma, his face bowed, and says nothing. Steadily he rises and puts his arms around her heaving shoulders. He holds her until her body settles.

My face swells with heat. I close my eyes, letting the tears drop violently on my lap. Auntie Maria and Betty are sobbing too. Their moans rise and fall in unison as if they're performing a weeping chorus.

"When I lost your father I thought my heart would stop, I thought you would bury me with him. I couldn't see how I could live without him. It happened suddenly, I was not prepared, and I was young then. I watched your sister die in front of me. And I couldn't help her. I couldn't help her, and I'm her mother." Ma wipes her face with the scarf around her shoulders, damp from all the tears. "I prayed every day for her to get better. I asked God, why not take me? I have done nothing for these children. Fikile deserves to live. I can die. What is my purpose in life?"

"I'm sorry, Ma."

"My son, my heart is sore. I don't have rest. God has taken away too much from me, I can't handle any more. It's enough now."

* * *

Mbuso and I are alone in the kitchen. Mbuso is leaning against the door surveying the kitchen's contents – everything is new to him except for the old Kelvinator fridge with its loud hum. I remember the day the fridge came in a large truck together with the Gommagommas and our parents' red velvet bedroom suite. We had just moved into our new house after my father spent many years extending the two-roomed structure. Ma glowed as she showed Auntie Betty the new furniture, how it snugged into place as if it were made for our house. In our "new big house", Fikile and I shared a room with two wrought iron single beds and matching bedspreads, separated by a wooden bed stand. We covered our walls with framed pictures of landscapes and faraway places we dreamt of travelling to, and heart-shaped collages with photographs of ourselves, family and friends. Mbuso slept on the small mattress on the floor in our parents' bedroom. The guest bedroom with its oversized gold satin comforter and matching pillows was off limits to us until Mbuso became too old for the mattress. My parents took pleasure acquiring items that with time filled our house – a broken but reparable floral lampshade from the neighbours of Ma's employers, a large mirror for our bathroom, a blue and white glass porcelain vase, a picture of Jesus washing his disciples' feet, which my father hung above the television in the family room.

I pour Mbuso cold water and offer him food. Mbuso takes the water and declines the food, says he is still full from the big lunch.

"Did Fikile suffer? Was she in a lot of pain?" he asks.

"Yes, it was difficult towards the end. Fikile hated that she couldn't walk, she said it was the worst punishment for her. She begged the universe to return her mobility."

"She was independent even as a child."

"And strong. Remember how Ma used to say Fikile was an ox in her other life, that she was always pulling and pulling."

"Ma was right."

"Well, the ox is gone. There's no one to pull us."

Mbuso places his arm on my shoulder and we stand there silent and blinking back tears.

"What about you, Mbuso? How are you?"

"I'm alright," he says, though his tone speaks of someone with a million thoughts. "Where is Thiza and the children?"

"The younger ones, Bafana and my daughter Mvula, are next door probably glued to the TV. Bafana threw a hysterical fit when Auntie Betty covered our TV and told them no one was allowed to turn it on. He said he wanted to go home. He hasn't lived in his house in months."

Mbuso raises his eyebrows, questioning.

"Fikile and the kids have been staying with us since she fell ill again. I will get them now-now, they will be happy to see you. They always ask about Uncle Mbuso. Lesihle thinks she remembers you but can't possibly, she was too young when you left. She is over there by the rocks, been sitting there the whole morning. I don't know what to do with her, maybe you can say something to her."

Mbuso looks out to where Lesihle is sitting. "She looks awful. What will I say to her?"

"You are her uncle, you will figure something out."

"And Khanya?"

"He is at Auntie Ntombi's, they will be here later. Auntie Ntombi said she has never witnessed such anguish as when she told Khanya about his mother. They were close, I called him Fikile's General. They went to war with Thiza many times; they didn't always win but fought nonetheless."

"And Thiza?"

"Nobody knows."

"He doesn't know?"

"Oh, he knows. He just hasn't showed his face." I look at Mbuso, long and hard. "Adjust your expectations, not much has changed here. Thiza is certainly as you know him."

"You mean, a *nonsonso*," Mbuso says in Ma's voice.

"Exactly." We pack up laughing and when the laughter dies Mbuso asks how I'm holding up.

I consider my brother's question for a moment. I don't know how to explain to him that I haven't had the indulgence to check my feelings in the hours since Fikile died, that the practicalities of preparing for a burial doesn't allow one time to do so. "It's been a tough year, but the worst is over, for now."

"I can imagine. I can't believe Fikile is gone."

"It was her time."

He nods and looks away.

"When is Mapule coming? How is she?"

Mbuso does not respond immediately. "She is not coming."

"She is not coming?"

"No."

"Why not?"

"We're going through a difficult time. She will not come."

"Mbuso, does she know Fikile died?"

"Yes, I told her."

"I don't understand why she's not here with us. This is so unlike Mapule. Should I call her?"

Mbuso shrugs, casually walks over to the sink to put down his empty glass.

"Mbuso, what is going on?"

I wait for an explanation.

When it becomes clear that my brother is not prepared to talk about his wife, I say, almost too brightly, "Okay. Okay." It is only then that I notice the absence of a wedding ring from his finger. Did the elders also see this or were they too blind with affection for the long-lost son? Our eyes meet, he sees that I've noticed the naked finger. "Come, let me show you to your room."

* * *

There are three brick rooms at the back of the main house, the back rooms. The rooms, each no bigger than a large-sized bathroom, are joined in a row. Each door is painted a bright colour, Sizwe's clever idea to distinguish among them. We refer to the rooms by their door colours: the red room, the yellow room, the blue room. Between the red and yellow room is a shared bathroom with a toilet, sink, and shower. I explain to Mbuso that we've kept the blue room for him. We had moved all his stuff from his old room inside the house in order to clear the space for Fikile after she fell ill the first time. The other two rooms are rented out to tenants.

"Does that mean I owe you rental income?"

"About four years' worth. We charge a thousand rand per room per month. You qualify for a small family discount."

"I'll have the cheque ready for you." Mbuso laughs.

"Ma refuses to let the room. She says she doesn't want you to feel like a visitor when you come home. She firmly believed that one day you would return home. And here you are."

I open the door and stand beside it. "All yours."

Mbuso takes a few steps and enters his room. I watch him move around the small space. "Feels as if I've entered a time capsule, I'm nineteen again." He opens the oak wardrobe, runs his hands through hanging, moth repellent-smelling clothes – torn jeans, shirts, an oversized and hole-riddled sweater of an American basketball team, caps with unrecognisable symbols and abbreviations. "You kept everything."

"Ma wouldn't let us touch anything, except for a few items she allowed Khanya to take. He sleeps here when he's around, he thinks you were cool in your youth."

Mbuso picks up an old notebook with his name drawn across in bold, black letters: his journal. He flips open a few pages and starts to laugh. "I don't know what to say."

"Say that you will stop acting like you don't have a home and a family who cares for you. Promise you won't disappear on us again."

"I promise."

"I'm serious."

Mbuso throws me one of his half smiles, the kind I know not to draw anything from.

"Ok, let me leave you to reminisce about the good old days, while I fetch the kids. I must warn you that Bafana is obsessed with cars. He will exhaust you with questions, and then will demand a ride to feel the horsepower. Sizwe, Mvula's father, is a car fanatic and guilty of fuelling Bafana's interest."

"Don't worry, I'll do whatever the young man wants. Mvula's father is around?"

"Yes, you will meet him. He should be here soon."

I leave Mbuso and join Ma and my aunts in the lounge.

"Where is Mapule? Where is our makoti?" Auntie Betty says, drawing out the makoti, our bride, in a taunt.

"She may not come."

A variation of gasps and murmurs.

"Why?" Ma asks, incredulous. "Why not? What did he say?"

"I don't know, Ma."

"I knew it, the boy hasn't changed." Auntie Betty claps her hands in anger.

"Give him a break, please, no wonder he left!"

*   *   *

Mbuso was our father's favourite child. Auntie Betty has narrated the story of how our father arrived home from work, smelling of sweat and diesel, the afternoon in late November Mbuso was born, and held the infant in his calloused hands.

"Umfana wami," he repeated until tears flowed from his eyes. To our father, the custodian of the Mabuza seed had arrived, unexpected yet the rightful, final piece of the puzzle, the circle of life complete. Over the days that followed, my father took pleasure in parading Mbuso to family members and friends, the traditional month-long waiting period ignored. Everyone fell in love with the boy.

But Ma was sick. She wouldn't breastfeed the baby despite the milk oozing out of her bulging breasts, leaving yellowish maps on her clothes. She wanted darkness and to rest her eyes; she refused to eat. When not asleep, she stared and stared into nothingness. Ma seemed scared of her own baby. Fikile and I had stayed away from her.

"*Jesus*, Margaret! What is wrong with you?" Auntie Betty would scoop the crying infant from the cot and rock him until he shut his eyes. "This is your boy. Aren't you happy you have given Meshack his boy at last?"

Ma's oldest sister, Auntie Betty, had been staying with us since she walked out of the convent where she spent half of her life as Sister Monica. I overhead her say to Ma that after helping so many women deliver babies she started to experience a yearning to become a mother too. She never did become a mother, though, because the man she was supposed to marry had vanished a night before his family was due to formally approach her family to begin talks of lobolo. Ma's family had prepared to welcome the groom's family – Mkhulu slaughtered a sheep and Gogo woke up early to cook her famous, fluffy dombolo and samp; my grandparents were proud of their eldest daughter. Ma said my aunt was so humiliated and heartbroken, she vowed not to let another man near her heart. She spent her years alone, working at the local clinic until she retired.

There were times when I caught Ma looking at baby Mbuso in a way that made me feel intense sadness for him. I wanted to protect him. By then I had decided that I did not wish to be my little brother. Even his soft curly hair that allowed the Afro comb to slide through without eliciting pain, the hair I was jealous of, and even the small pink penis that had drawn the line between our father and us – my sister and I – casting us off our coveted spot in our father's arms, seemed too much of a price to pay. Auntie

Ntombi, Ma's youngest sister, had said Ma was suffering from the trauma of having another boy and was afraid to lose him too. Fikile was not our parents' first child, Auntie had said, Mbuso was not the first boy in the family.

Our first brother died before he was born. When we were alone with Auntie Ntombi, Fikile had asked for his name. She said he died before he was named. For days, Fikile and I spoke about our dead older brother, five years older than Fikile. We debated his name – Mandla, the strong one, Fikile's choice, and Simphiwe, our gift, mine – the colour of his skin, height, preference for boxing like our father. We agreed he would not fear the boys and girls who sometimes took our pocket money and beat us, and concluded that life would be much better if he was around. Because my brother died before he was fully formed, our parents could not bury him, Auntie Ntombi said when Fikile asked to visit his grave. Ma never spoke about him, and with time, we forgot about him.

My father's love for Mbuso was plentiful, as if to compensate for Ma's lack of affection. I watched them with envy: a four-month-old Mbuso at his baptism, draped in white, crying on my father's arm; a gleeful Mbuso clumsily scooping up the fat rainbow-coloured candle, shaped in the form of number one, from the blue, frosted cake my father brought home for his first birthday; Mbuso, at four, falling off his brand-new tricycle and my father urging him to get back on. Mbuso rode and rode until he thought he was flying.

And then my father died. Mbuso was five.

The troublesome times with Mbuso came soon after he

91

turned fifteen. He was in grade nine, and had, until that year, been an exceptional student, his teachers' favourite; well behaved for a boy raised without "proper" parental guidance, the teachers commented. The same teachers noticed the change. Mr Khuzwayo, Mbuso's Mathematics teacher and Fikile's fellow church member, took Fikile aside after church one Sunday. He wanted to know if there was new trouble at home. Mbuso had not been in class the entire week, he said. "I thought I should ask if there were difficulties preventing him from attending. He is a good student, one of our best, we are naturally concerned for him." There was something else, Mr Khuzwayo continued, had we noticed his grades were falling? For two consecutive quarters he was not at the top of his class, not even in the top ten.

Fikile came straight home after church. Mbuso and I had long abandoned the idea of religion, stopped believing that the Holy Trinity could do anything for us. We had prayed for years for Ma's recovery without results.

"We have a problem," she said, proceeding to Mbuso's room. "Is he in?" Fikile did not wait for my response. She tapped once at his door and turned the handle. The door was unlocked. I followed her inside.

Mbuso's room smelled of his unwashed body and mould and stale alcohol. I pinched my nose and stood by the door.

"Mbuso, wake up." Fikile threw open the curtains and windows letting in the light, air. "How many days has he locked himself up like this? Is he even eating? Anele, why haven't you said anything? How can you let this happen?"

I darted my eyes around Mbuso's room, full of guilt. I had not paid close attention to my brother in recent months, too swallowed up in my own discontentment to notice the digression. Mbuso had appeared fine to me.

A confused Mbuso, eyes burning red, head in his hands, attempted to sit upright. "What do you want?"

"Is this how you greet me now?" Fikile looked down at him with weary tenderness.

Mbuso grunted something between a curse and a greeting.

"I hear you've stopped going to school."

"Why does it matter to you?"

I held my breath. Fikile spoke and we obeyed, that was the order of things. I expected her to leap onto him and smack some sense into his head, instead she crossed the room and sat next to Mbuso. She spoke softly to him, her voice guarded. "What's wrong?" When Mbuso did not answer, Fikile continued, "You know you can talk to me about anything, right?"

"I'm sick of school. I'm sick of being here," Mbuso roared, catching Fikile off guard.

"What do you want to do, move out?"

I frowned at my sister, why was she bargaining with Mbuso?

Mbuso stared at Fikile. I could tell he had not expected that question. "Just leave me alone."

"No, leaving you alone is not an option. You are either going back to school or moving out. Your choice."

Mbuso stared at his feet.

"We are trying here, Mbuso. Life is not easy for any of us. Please don't skip school, otherwise you will end up in the streets with no future."

"You mean no future like Anele? I sure don't want that," he hissed under his breath.

"That's not fair," I protested.

"Forget Anele," Fikile yelled at him. "You have your own life to live, Mbuso, your own future to look forward to."

"What's unfair is that I was born into a family of losers. I wish Dad was here," he said.

"We also wish Baba was here, but he's not. Deal with it."

"Anele, please," Fikile said.

"No, I won't keep quiet. I put my dreams on hold for you and what do I receive as thanks? A bucket of bullshit. Let me tell you, boy, I could leave this place anytime."

"Why don't you?"

"Because of you, idiot."

"Anele! Mbuso! Enough, both of you."

Mbuso never got over his disappointment with me for changing my mind about leaving home, he saw this as a personal betrayal. In our parentless state, after Fikile had moved in with Thiza, my brother and I spent hours plotting our escape to build a life far away from home. I would get a bursary to study medicine, no, accounting – Mbuso argued that medical school took too long. I would find a job that paid well with a big investment bank, and then I would come for him. We would live a beautiful life filled with books and movies and concerts, and go on hiking trips to the mountains or camping in small tents. Just us. Mbuso would finish his matric and fly off to study in America, the first person in our family to get on a plane, to cross oceans. When the dream had not materialised, after I chose to stay closer to home, with an inventory of menial jobs – packing groceries, selling cane furniture, managing office receptions – and study by mail to keep an eye on him and Ma, Mbuso had raged.

"Why don't you come stay –" Fikile stopped herself. She wanted to say, why don't you come stay with us for a while, but knew Mbuso would only laugh at her. A year before, Mbuso had spent a few days with them. Thiza, excited to have an older boy in the house, made the mistake of taking Mbuso everywhere he went. The unimpressionable Mbuso witnessed the man he respected and loved like a father get drunk to the point of passing out and turn himself into the township's laughing stock. The first time it happened, he had not said anything to Fikile, not even when she poked for their whereabouts. "Where were you? What did you do? Who was there? Was it only Thiza and his friends? What did you eat, drink?" The second time, Mbuso drove his brother-in-law home, car in third gear doing forty kilometres per hour. He handed the car keys to a perplexed Fikile and said, "Your husband is a joke." He then collected his belongings and walked home in the middle of the night.

"I can't wait to leave this dump. You all make me sick." Mbuso turned his back to face the wall, signalling the end of the conversation.

"You can leave if you want." Fikile stood and walked out.

"You are a thankless bastard," I jeered at him and followed Fikile.

"I don't know what to do anymore," Fikile was crying. I hadn't seen my sister's eyes wet in years.

"I'll look after him, I promise."

A few days later Mbuso slit his wrist and tried to cover it up. I had taken to conducting daily raids in his room using the spare key when he was out. I found a bundle of bloodied towels and a long-sleeved shirt under his bed. Panicked, I called Auntie Betty. We waited for Mbuso to return. Auntie Betty cleaned up Mbuso's wounds, which were oozing pus, with warm water and an antiseptic solution, and bandaged them. We called Uncle Majaha. I sat with the elders as they spoke to Mbuso. They had clear intentions, yet when they spoke, coaxing Mbuso to empty his chest, their voices lacked the firmness I had expected. There was a general nervousness in how they treaded carefully around their son's volatile temper. Auntie Ntombi offered to take him, Mbuso refused and promised to clean up his act.

Mbuso failed his mid-year exams that year.

For a few months Mbuso appeared to have changed his ways, that is until the fallout with Ma. There was no provocation I could think of, Mbuso's fury flowed spontaneously as if he had a special place in his heart from where he could fetch it at a moment's notice. There was, however, a silent agreement that existed between him and Ma: Ma was forbidden from speaking to him, her voice alone was enough to trigger an avalanche of insults from my younger brother. What I recall about that day is my brother viciously lunging at Ma like a bulldog, the loud thud of her bum hitting the concrete floor, his scrawny body on top of hers, years of anger wrapped in his fists landing one after the other like a Highveld hailstorm.

It happened so fast. I tugged at Mbuso's shirt, trying to pull him away. "Mbuso, don't kill her! Mbuso, don't! Please, stop!"

"My son. My son. I'm your mother. I'm –" Ma's muffled pleas, hands over her face, blood gushing from her nose and mouth, dripping down her neck. Her head wrap came undone, covering part of her face. Her dress rolled up to her midriff, exposing frayed beige panties. A small pool of blood gathered on the floor.

Mbuso did not utter a word as he unleashed his blows.

"Mbuso, stop!" I was crying, Ma was being beaten to death in front of me and I couldn't help her.

As swiftly as the beating had started, it stopped. Mbuso rose, pushed me aside, and stormed out of the house.

Ma was a bloody mess; she had sustained a deep cut above her left eye.

I called Fikile, who came with Thiza. We took Ma to the local clinic.

"What happened?"

"It was an accident," Ma said before Fikile and I could respond.

The nurse worked carefully around the cut, nine stitches.

Ma did not once moan from pain, she closed and opened her eye as instructed. Ma's left eye was severely injured. The nurse placed cotton on it and bandaged the eye and told us to take her to the hospital the following day.

"What really happened?" the nurse asked again. "Because if this is a case of abuse, then you must report it to the police." She turned briefly to look at Fikile and I, eyebrows raised as if to say, *You're with me here, right?* "Men get away with murder and we, us, women, allow them to. Yesterday a woman died here. Her husband split her in half and ripped out her insides. The madness needs to stop." She sighed aloud to release her frustration and left the room.

Mbuso's cell phone was turned off. We searched all over for him, nobody had seen him. On the second day of his disappearance, we reported him missing at the local police station. The boy will return, give him time, you know boys are boys, the officer in charge of the case said. As we were leaving the police station we heard the officers laugh. "I wonder what the mother did to get such a lashing. *Eish*, boys," someone commented.

I couldn't sleep. Ma wouldn't leave the house, her pain and anxiety unmistakable amid her bluish face. "You still can't get hold of him?" she asked every few minutes. "Shouldn't you go back to the police? My son. What if he never comes back to us? What will I say to your father?"

Fikile cried, claimed all the responsibility.

Mbuso returned home late on the evening of the fifth day. I was up waiting for him as I had done since he left.

Ma was asleep on the couch, an empty bottle of beer on the coffee table. I heard the kitchen door key turn, the creaky sound of the door opening, a firm close.

"Mbuso?" I jumped up from my seat. I met him in the passageway, his eyes refused to lift to mine. I turned without speaking to him, went to fetch our mother, and put her to bed. That evening I slept.

Mbuso woke up early the following morning and waited for me in the kitchen.

"I'm sorry," he said.

"You need to apologise to your mother."

When Ma made her way to the kitchen a few minutes later, clutching her head from a hangover, her one eye still covered, Mbuso's face tensed. She cried all over him, apologising for her failures, accepting the beating as a deserved punishment. Mbuso watched her with disgust, and walked away.

Mbuso went to school that day, and for the years that followed poured all his anger into his books. He said nothing about where he'd been, and no one asked him anything.

To his credit and against all his demons, Mbuso was smart enough to set aside his rebellion during his matric year, work hard, such that when his results came out, a litany of distinctions, two top universities offered him a full bursary to study engineering.

We were so elated by Mbuso's achievements that Thiza organised an impromptu braai. Ma cried. Fikile had cashed up the little education policy taken by our father to buy him university supplies, decent linen, a phone, two pairs of jeans, a few T-shirts, and running shoes. He was a progressive man, my father, even in those days, planning for our education when he had got no further than standard six.

Throughout Mbuso's first year, Auntie Ntombi sent him pocket money, a task she assumed without anyone asking and without expecting anything in return. She had been lucky to receive an education, she said, she understood the sacrifices made by her father and older sisters. When Auntie Ntombi was starting high school – Ma married and with a small child, Fikile, and Auntie Betty living in the convent – the two sisters had pulled together whatever funds they could to take her out of their dilapidated house on the farm where their father had worked almost all his life, and sent her to a Catholic boarding school.

During his second year of studies, Mbuso wrote a polite letter to Auntie Ntombi thanking her for her support, and announcing that he had found himself a job off campus tutoring matriculants in Mathematics and Science, and that the pay was good enough for him not to need her stipends anymore. It was the year he stopped coming home.

the ones with purpose are dying

Because Fikile was a married woman, the funeral proceedings will be conducted from her matrimonial home. It is at stand number 22 Andrew Mlangeni Street where every day we will temporarily uproot our lives, filling every corner of the house with our bodies and belongings and talk. Where we will invoke Fikile's memories and those of other dead family members, and where we will welcome friends and neighbours and strangers who have come to show solidarity with us.

Mbuso and I drive out to prepare Fikile's place to receive the aggrieved. I last went there two months ago to fetch the rest of the children's clothes and toys. By then it was evident that Fikile was losing the fight, she was dying but we didn't know when, and there was nothing left for anyone to do except wait.

The Dlamini house stands proud in this coveted part of our location, Bright City section. It is among the first face-brick houses built back when the people were dizzy with dreams and optimism of a better life, the taste of freedom still fresh and sweet. Thiza had bought the house with his first wife, Lindiwe, way before Fikile entered the picture, stamping her mark, and changing the chain of events, altering destinies. I remember Sir Dlamini and Miss Lindiwe's wedding as one of the grandest of the time. Everyone in

New Hope attended and people spoke about it for months. The bride looked like a doll with her pink cheeks and hair pulled up in a neat, braided bun. Lindiwe had surprised her guests by changing into three wedding gowns, a first for New Hope. There were cars too, big cars with tops pulled down, revealing slick black interiors. We ululated and ululated and ate and drank sweet juice and danced until dusk, when our parents started calling our names in the crowd and told us it was time to go home.

The first time Fikile brought me inside the house – showing me around like she had been part of the equation from the beginning, from when the foundation was laid, rooms painted, and furniture selected – was shortly after Lindiwe left. I didn't know Thiza's wife had moved back with her family. I followed Fikile in and out of the different rooms, exquisitely decorated as if the owners had spent copious amounts of time consulting home decorating magazines or watching decorating shows on television. My head jerked at the slightest movement outside, my heart raced with concern that Thiza's wife would walk in on us and demand to know why we were floating around in her house like we belonged there. Fikile must have sensed my unease.

"Lindiwe no longer lives here," she said matter-of-factly. "This is mine now."

Mbuso stops the car, climbs out to open the padlock, and slides open the bronze-painted metal gate, adorned with the image of a tiger. He leaves his car under the carport next to the garage. Fikile initially used the garage as a classroom for her crèche. I can still hear the full laughter of Fikile's children, their tiny voices reciting the Lord's Prayer, Fikile chanting along and cheering them on. We follow a paved walkway to the back of the house where strands of ivy have crept from the garden and forced their way through the walls, window frames, and under the kitchen door.

"Doesn't look like anyone has lived here for a while," Mbuso exclaims as he starts pulling the wild plant from the door, piling the leaves to one side.

"Thiza was hardly home even when Fikile was still here," I say, letting us through the door. When Sizwe and I were last here, he emptied the garbage bin, the contents of which had begun to rot, while I tidied up and washed the few dishes in the sink. The house was showing signs of sporadic inhabitation.

Except for the musty smell of unventilated space and wafts of alcohol and cigarettes, the house is in a decent condition. My head buzzes with memories as we move from the kitchen to the lounge and dining room, the narrow passage leading to the bedroom, the boys' room to the right, Lesihle's to the left, and finally to Fikile and Thiza's bedroom. I pick up Thiza's crumpled shirt and pants on the floor of the bathroom and toss them in the laundry bin behind the door.

"Beautiful house," Mbuso says, moving around the room, inspecting every corner. "They must have spent a fortune renovating, I barely recognise anything here. Where did they get the money to do all of this?"

"Thiza's pension. Fikile wanted them to renovate the kitchen and bathroom, do minor touches here and there, and invest the rest of the money. Thiza told her it was his money and he could do with it as he pleased. And that's exactly what he did – pressed ceilings, marble countertops, carved doors. For what, when today he is broker than a cheap joke?"

"Why did he leave teaching?"

"He raped a girl, one of his students."

"Jesus!" Mbuso exclaims, holding his head. "When was this?"

"Years back, probably shortly after you left."

Everybody knows it was the rape claim that pushed Thiza into early retirement, and not the need to explore new opportunities, follow the gravy train of empowerment as he preferred to explain. The family of the girl, a grade nine student, were seething. The mediated efforts of the school principal, Mr Dube, Thiza's childhood friend and fellow appreciator of girls barely out of puberty, were met with scornful faces and calls for justice. Thiza may have got away with his deeds before, but not this time, not their child, the family said.

"The family pressed charges. Thiza was arrested. He paid bail. Then resigned. The department paid him his pension, a lump sum. The case disappeared."

"I can't believe it."

"What, that he forced himself onto a child or the case disappearing?"

"Both I guess, I'm shocked. Thiza?"

"It wasn't the first time your brother-in-law took advantage of a young woman. His whole life has been about that, our sister is a case in point."

"I forget how young Fikile was when she got into those shenanigans with him. What did Fikile do about his case?"

"Fikile did what she always did, she left him, moved back home with Khanya and Lesihle. Thiza did what he always did, came begging for her forgiveness; he was an absolute wreck. She took him back on condition he got help, and so for a while Thiza was attending counselling to deal with his *condition*. Jail was more befitting in my view but he had money then and could buy his freedom."

"So where is he now?"

"Shacking up with someone."

Mbuso looks at me in utter disbelief, shakes his head.

"I actually think this arrangement is good for him, how else is he going to survive? Thiza doesn't have money, you will see how pathetic he looks. It took him three years to squander his pension money; fourteen years of service wasted on aimless business ventures, alcohol, and funding pre-paid airtime, cheap girl clothes and plastic hair. The two shops he built as part of his empire, as he boasted, are in such a state of disrepair. He is renting them out to Pakistanis who call him Big Boss T and allow him to loot packs of illegal cigarettes at the end of the month when he comes to collect rent. The red BMW, a stark reminder of glory days, has spent more days at the back of Titus's Auto Garage than on the road. At the age of forty-four, Thiza has managed to screw up his life, fast and furious. That's the story of your brother-in-law."

"I can't believe Fikile stayed with him for as long as she did."

"For a while she was down in that hole with him. They survived on the commission she made selling storage containers and dishes, stainless steel pots, cosmetics, tablecloths, cleaning products, health products, you name it. But it's what married people do, isn't it? Stay. Through ups and downs, shit or sugar, that's what Fikile said."

"Not always."

"I wouldn't know."

"You don't have to be married to know."

I watch him pick up a photograph of Fikile in the frame by the bedstand, smooth a finger over it – Fikile is running from a wave and smiling shyly at the camera as she often did when attention was directed at her.

"The photo was taken last year, our last holiday together after her cancer came back. The children were so happy to see the sea. We became water babies in that week, swimming every morning and afternoon. Let me rephrase that, the kids and Sizwe swam, Fikile and I waddled in the waves. A bittersweet moment; I cried when no one was looking. Fikile put on a brave face. You can't tell by looking at her that she only had months to live."

"The doctors told you that?"

"They don't quite put it in those words." Her oncologist was polite, said Fikile didn't have long to live. I was the one who poked, how long is long – ten years? Five years? Two years? The doctor shook her head each time. A year? If we are lucky, she said in the most desperate voice I've ever heard. The world caved in, and all I could see was a deep, dark hole. When I came to, I was lying on the doctor's couch, Fikile's face hovering over me. "You can't die before me," Fikile said.

Mbuso puts the frame down, exhales deeply.

"Don't start." I wave him off.

He leaves the bedroom. I hear him blow his nose. He is quiet for some time. When he is done collecting his emotions, he moves to other rooms, opening and closing doors. I hear whistles.

There is another photo of Fikile, holding a graduation gown in her arm. She is wearing a long-sleeved cobalt blue dress with lace flounce. She looks beautiful and regal, the delicate lace against her dark skin. As far as I know Fikile wore the dress only that one time. I was surprised by her choice, certainly not the type my sister would choose for herself, too extravagant and short for her "banana" legs, as she referred to them. I walk over to Fikile's closet, swing the doors open wide, and start searching through the hangers for the dress. I decide to bury my sister in the blue dress; I'm certain she would have chosen the same herself.

The dress is not among those lining the closet. I comb through drawers, reach for top shelves, under the bed, but it isn't there. I'm about to go search in Lesihle's room when I notice a brown box shoved at the back of the closet. I pick up the box and empty its contents on the bed. The dress is neatly folded together with the black gown and a silver sash. There is a pair of black platform shoes and a smaller box with pearl earrings – everything Fikile wore on her graduation. A few photographs of Fikile's graduation escape and land on the floor, I pick them up one by one. Most are of Fikile, except for one of a man I do not recognise. I turn the photo over, nothing.

I look up, Mbuso is standing by the door.

"What are those?"

"Old pictures of Fikile's graduation."

"You okay, sisi?"

"Please give me a minute, I want to say my goodbyes. Fikile and I spent many hours in this room, lying on this bed."

"Of course, take your time." Mbuso closes the door behind him and walks out of the house. I hear his footsteps in the garden, the scraping of a shovel.

Alone, I take off my shoes and lie on Fikile's side of the bed, the side closest to the window. Fikile liked to open the window and curtains first thing in the morning, she said the sun gave her hope; I hated the habit when we were young and shared a room. I squeeze the pillow and run my fingers on the soft satin pillow. Fikile had signed up with a catalogue company to sell linen, satin duvets with matching pillowcases and continental pillowcases, but ended up liking the set so much she spent a year paying it off. Without warning, tears sharp and plentiful flood my eyes and pour down my cheeks. I don't stop them. I have not allowed myself a moment to sit down, to grieve. Being with Fikile throughout her illness had denied me the privilege of mourning.

I don't know how long I stay curled up on Fikile's bed or for how long I doze off. When I open my eyes, Mbuso is gently shaking me, calling my name.

"We must go. Auntie Betty called."

"I will miss her," I say.

"You've always been close. Sometimes I was jealous, wished I had a brother."

"We only fought once. Terrible fight. We did not speak to each other for days. I was sixteen and had started secretly seeing some guy in matric. I knew Fikile wouldn't be pleased if she found out, you know how she was always on our case about getting good grades and education?"

Mbuso laughs, and says, "Don't remind me."

"So I didn't tell her, which was difficult because I shared everything with her. Somehow, she found out. I came home one afternoon, inexcusably late, and found her in the kitchen. I knew I was in trouble. I walked in, made small talk to test the waters. Fikile didn't say a word to me, she landed a single klap on my right cheek. I stood there, stars dancing in my eyes, hand over my cheek, the room around me reeling. I think we were both shocked, Fikile had never laid a finger on me or you. She said: Continue seeing that boy and you will see, there are many more where that klap came from. She turned to the pot as if nothing had happened. I don't know what came over me, but I sprang onto her screaming that she was not my mother, how I hated her, who was she to tell me who I could or could not date when she was fooling around with a teacher and a married man. I may have called her a whore."

Mbuso winces. "You crossed the line there."

"When you are sixteen you think you know everything. Fikile turned from the stove, gave me another solid klap on the same cheek, pushed me aside to feed Khanya who had started crying. My two cents of boldness was no match, I backed off, took whatever was left of my dignity to my room and sobbed to myself. I didn't speak to her for several days. I avoided her or gave her dirty looks. Fikile wasn't fazed by my performance, she carried on as if nothing had happened. Eventually I couldn't take the silence between us, I apologised. She made it clear that she would beat me until I stopped the nonsense I was doing with the guy. We started talking again."

"I don't remember any of this."

"You were young and still a good boy."

Mbuso's face darkens. He shifts his gaze from me.

"I'm sorry, I don't mean it like that."

"I know. Fikile tried with us."

"She did."

I fold the dress, put it in the box and inside the closet.

"I've cleaned up what I could, I will fix the garden after the funeral. We can't leave Fikile's house looking like a bush," Mbuso says.

We rearrange the furniture in the lounge, and place Fikile's mattress on the floor against the wall by the corner furthest from the door. It is in this room, in the small space between the mattress and the wall, where Fikile's thawing body will lie in a coffin among those who loved her, the night before she is buried.

I lock the house, wait for Mbuso to reverse out of the yard, and slide closed the gate before snapping its lock shut. We drive home to fetch Ma and Auntie Betty and the children to begin the vigil.

*   *   *

Thiza's mother, Mama Dlamini, arrives accompanied by Thiza's older brother, Thulani. He helps her out of the car, hooks her frail arm onto his while balancing the other on her walking stick, and leads her inside the house. She finds Ma and Auntie Betty lumped on Fikile's mattress, drinking black tea, and ready to receive mourners. They are ready to sit in this position until Fikile is buried. Ma has wrapped a black scarf around her head, and draped a black shawl over her shoulders. She looks properly bereaved. The gigantic flat-screen television set mounted on the wall has been covered with a white tablecloth. A faint smell of incense wafts through the room. Auntie Betty makes room for Mama Dlamini on the mattress.

"Fikile is the reason I'm alive today. The Lord may as well take me too, I have nothing to live for. Better those who are long resting and spared from this agony." Her grief swells up and fills the room, her voice is a raw moan of pain. Mama Dlamini is well into her eighties, her eyesight is starting to go.

When Fikile sneaked into the Dlamini's lives, young and unwavering and with evidence of fertility, Mama Dlamini opened her arms wide for her and little Khanya. Mama Dlamini pursed her lips and threw her hands in the air in a manner that said: "Who am I to judge God's way?" when friends and neighbours commented on the surprising additions. Or was Thiza planning to take a second wife?

Fikile queued for hours at the hospital each month to collect Ma and Mama Dlamini's diabetes and high blood pressure medicines, took Mama Dlamini to the bank to draw her pension money and to the shopping plaza to buy groceries and occasionally shop for underwear and a skirt, a shirt, a jersey at JetMart. They frequented the local market by the taxi rank where on Thursdays they stocked up on amadumbe, raw peanuts for the pumpkin leaves stew, spinach, dry beans, and beef bones for the soup. Mama Dlamini delighted in their monthly trips to the casino where they played the ten-cent slots until their heads buzzed with the rolling sounds and jingles from the surrounding winning machines.

I join Auntie Betty in the kitchen. She has taken up the task of cooking a large pot of porridge and tomato chutney to go with the boiled chicken.

"I wish I could wave a magic wand to wipe away Mama Dlamini's pain, she makes me sad," I say.

"Fikile was practically her daughter. Anyone would be distraught to lose someone like her."

"I'm worried for her. How will she cope without Fikile? She has no one, no offence but I don't see Thiza or Thulani checking on her."

"They will have to, she is their mother."

I shake my head. "Not those two."

"Now, listen to me, young lady. Mama Dlamini is not a load to burden yourself with. She is not your problem. She has her own people who can look after her."

"I'm only saying –"

"I know you and your charitable heart. You have enough on your plate as it is, there are four kids who will be looking up to you and demanding your attention, demanding to be fed, clothed, educated and taken to everything that children do these days, swimming lessons and soccer. Don't try to be both yourself and Fikile, it's not your job to fill her shoes."

"Fine, Aunt."

"I mean it, I don't want you to concern yourself about Thiza's mother's welfare. I don't want to hear you mention her again, okay?"

"I hear you."

"Where is your brother?"

"Outside, resting. He is exhausted from the drive."

"And from his troubles. I don't understand this solitary life he has chosen for himself, how do you go on as if you don't belong anywhere?" She places the wooden spoon on the side of the pot, reduces the heat. "Majaha is right, Mbuso needs umsebenzi."

"Why?"

"He is clearly troubled, he needs cleansing."

I laugh at my aunt. "Since when do we cleanse people here?"

"We can always start. I'm telling you, something's not right with your brother."

"Can you blame him for how he has turned out? Mbuso did what was best for him at the time. We were too dysfunctional, offered him no hope. At least Fikile and I had something to hold on to – Dad's memory. I think that is what kept us going all those years, knowing what normality looked like. Our brother had nothing; he only knew poverty and disappointment and broken dreams."

Auntie Betty narrows her eyes, stares at me like I'm poison. "Why are you so set on defending your brother's despicable actions? You're starting to get on my nerves. How do you think your mother feels? Margaret hurts for that child. Every day he is out there doing who knows what, your mother sits here heartbroken. Why do you think she took so long to overcome her addiction? She is bottling all that hurt."

"I'm not defending anyone. Family has a way of weighing you down, placing your dreams on pause, sometimes indefinitely. Auntie, look at Fikile and how we *happened* upon her life and completely derailed her journey."

"It's family, we all have responsibility towards family."

"Exactly my point. Why should we be held back by family?

I didn't ask to be born, why must I inherit something I did not choose to be part of from the beginning?"

"What are you saying, Anele?"

I do not say to my aunt to consider that the same has *happened* to me, that I've instantly become a mother of three more children, that even with Ma's sobriety and new optimism, I could never dare leave them alone with her. I don't say it's easy for you to speak, you choose your involvements, you choose when to turn away from it all and go home to your life. My thoughts are of course unfair towards my aunt; she – like Fikile and I – knows first-hand the responsibility of family.

"Fikile got a raw deal out of life. Sometimes I wish I had my brother's attitude, I'll be far in life. Mbuso chose himself."

"And is he happy? Do you look at him and think, 'I want his life'? Do you? Your life is far richer and more fulfilled than that brother of yours. Say what you may but I just see sadness. I hope my sister's child finds a way to stop fighting with himself. Pass me the tomatoes."

* * *

Reverend Madida, accompanied by a handful of church members, arrives late in the afternoon. There is silence as they file into the house, occupying every chair in the room. The minister is in his usual black gear with a white collar, a small red ribbon attached to the front pocket of his jacket. Each member is adorned with a purple item, mostly blouses for the ladies, ribbons for the men. Purple is the church's

117

colour. Fikile, too, owned several shirts in varying shades of purple.

Reverend Madida speaks, they are returning from a funeral of a fellow church member – the reason they were not able to come earlier. Stroke. So young. A policeman, a whole captain, a good one at that, not a sniff of corruption to his name. The ones with purpose are dying, he says, who will be left to save this world?

He is a popular minister in the area, educated with an Advanced Diploma in Theology obtained from a legitimate school of theology. "I am the real deal, not some fly-by-night pastor. Know your shepherds, the wolves are plentiful out there."

Reverend Madida leads his members in a chorus, and begins his sermon by reading a verse from the Bible. His baritone voice, toned down a few decibels for the occasion, sends a series of vibrations into the crowded room, eliciting a string of excited groans, Amens! and Hallelujahs!

The sermon comes to an end.

Reverend Madida releases his members but remains behind to round off the funeral arrangements. I bring juice and biscuits, something small for the man of God.

Fikile did not want a night vigil. We agree to hold a service after her body arrives late Friday afternoon. The following day's agenda is finalised.

"Short and sweet, no fuss, exactly how Fikile would have wanted it," Reverend Madida adds.

* * *

There are more people at the door, the mourning period has officially begun. They move inside silently, only the scraping of chairs gives them away. From the kitchen I listen as the mourners take their seats. One person launches into a gospel chorus, the others join in, humming, their soothing voices filling the room. Someone starts to cry, soft sobs that develop into full-blown howls. Ma? I lean in, worried for her; Fikile has only been dead for a few hours, there are six days to go before she is buried.

i won't be here for you forever

Mbuso and I are sitting at the back of Fikile's house. Mbuso is impatiently swatting mosquitoes.

"That's what happens when you leave home for too long, even the local pests don't recognise you," I tease him as I hand over the mosquito repellent.

"That's not true," he retorts. "These buggers have always hated me. It's a wonder I did not die from malaria. Remember that time we went on the school trip to the game reserve and I came back, my arms and legs lumpy like the dough I used to make when we baked? Fikile rushing me to the clinic, scared I would break into malaria fever? Remember that?"

"You were seven or eight. You had us in a panic. Later that year, you learned about malaria at school, its causes and symptoms. You couldn't wait to tell Fikile about it."

"Fikile tried to look after us. She did well considering she was a child herself."

Fikile became our mother a year after the accident that killed our father. I know exactly the day my sister took over our household, the day Ma's employers, the Hopkinses – very nice people from America who had come to our country to start a rhino sanctuary – let her go after they found her sleeping on the sofa holding a nip of brown liquor, the baby playing with her toys in soiled nappies that had started to ooze out, and the house engulfed in a putrid funk. We later learned this was the second incident of this nature.

Mrs Hopkins brought Ma home in her large white van, its body plastered with thick mud. She pulled up in our yard and called out for someone, anyone, to come and help her. Fikile, Mbuso and I rushed out of the house to see Ma staggering out of the van, ignoring Mrs Hopkins's plea to wait for assistance. She passed us without saying a word, and went inside the house. We trailed behind, Mrs Hopkins followed at a short distance. In her bedroom Ma threw herself on the bed and went straight to sleep. We stood by the door watching her.

I had not seen Mrs Hopkins in a long time, and even when I had seen her our interactions happened from the rolled-down window of her car and were fleeting – a smile or wink, a pat of my Afro, a hurried enquiry about my school performance. She had come inside our house only once before. Before our father's death, only Mbuso had spent time with the Hopkinses, though he had recoiled and hid behind Fikile's dress when Mrs Hopkins opened her arms, expecting a hug. Mbuso had come down with pneumonia, and after the third day of his cough refusing to subside – even after Ma came home early and took him to the clinic – Mrs Hopkins wanted to take him to her doctor in town. Mbuso spent a night with the Hopkinses, and eventually recovered, and for weeks spoke of riding in Mrs Hopkins's car and playing with their dog, Santos. How he was initially afraid of the dog, until the dog started to lick him and how he was not afraid of it anymore after that.

At first I didn't recognise Mrs Hopkins when she brought Ma home, her skin had turned leathery and brown for a white woman and she was dripping with sweat. She wasn't at all like the snowy white women I saw on television and in magazines, women with doll hair so white and whippy I dreamt of touching it. Mrs Hopkins's hair looked the colour of dirt and it was tangled like our jump rope. However, when she spoke – her voice as if coming from the bottom of her nasal passages – she was a white woman.

Mrs Hopkins gave Ma one last look, shook her head, and left the room. We followed her. Outside, Mbuso and I flanked Fikile like guards and watched Mrs Hopkins. We had taken to clustering about my sister, a habit that irritated her but she did not shoo us away. Maybe she too was a little scared.

"You understand this is not what we want. We love Margaret very much. Baby Samantha will be heartbroken. She adores your mother," Mrs Hopkins said. "This is not easy for us. I hope you understand. We thought if we gave her another chance she would come right, we understand the pressure of raising young children on your own." Mrs Hopkins gestured towards Mbuso and me. I was fascinated by how she kept saying "we", "us", though she was the only one present. My teacher had explained the use of singular versus plural pronouns, surely Mrs Hopkins, who should have known better, was breaking the rules. I kept quiet.

Mrs Hopkins asked Fikile to walk with her towards the car where she took out plastic bags full of clothes. "Something to tide you over while Margaret looks for another job, mostly Samantha's clothes, good clothes, some hardly worn. The young ones grow up so fast! I've also thrown in a few of mine and John's, should fetch a few hundred rands at the market, enough for groceries for a couple of weeks?" Then she pulled out a plump brown envelope, leaned over to Fikile and spoke in a hushed tone. "I want you to keep this money safe. It's for your uniforms and stationery. I don't want you to use it on anything else but school, you hear?" She clasped Fikile's hands around the envelope. "And I don't want your mother to find this money because we both know what she would do with it, right?"

Fikile nodded.

With an air of someone troubled, Mrs Hopkins sighed again and promised to check on us soon. We watched her walk towards her car and drive off. We never saw Mrs Hopkins again.

I asked Fikile if she was going to open the envelope. She shrugged and said okay, and made us go in the garage in case Ma woke up. We counted the crisp ten, twenty and fifty rand notes, my eyes widening with each hundred rand counted.

"Six hundred rand," I whispered, impressed.

Fikile clicked her tongue and said it was not much; she said Ma had worked for the Hopkinses from when I was a toddler.

The following morning Fikile took a taxi to town, bought groceries, electricity, and underwear for Mbuso and I. She only returned home after we ate dinner of leftover pap and potato cabbage, and whispered in my ear that she was going to take care of us. What was left of the money she deposited into her Post Office bank account which our father had opened. He had taken a special day off from work and drove us to town to open accounts for each of us. On the way, our father educated us on the importance of money and saving and patience. He made an example of our home, how he and Ma had poured out their sweat and tears, labouring daily and putting away every cent towards extending the house and how it eventually paid off. I remember sitting quietly soaking in every word. Fikile asked questions. Mbuso bounced off his seat and occupied himself with his toy soldier. We left the post office beaming, our savings documents secured in Ma's handbag. After our parents had finished with their other errands and Mbuso's crankiness had reached unbearable levels, we went to buy fried chicken and chips which we ate under a tree a few kilometres outside of town.

After losing her job with the Hopkinses, Ma locked herself in her bedroom for four nights. She wouldn't eat or wash, and only sipped on water in the glass by her bed. She kept the curtains shut. Sometimes she cried, sorrowful sobs that hummed through the walls to every corner of the house. She spoke in monotones, said no more than a few words at a time. Auntie Betty moved in with us again. She said Ma had returned to life too soon after our father's death, before her heart was completely healed and before much of the grief had poured out of her system. Fikile and I took turns bringing Ma tea and bread only to remove it an hour later untouched. We knew well enough to keep out of Ma's way when her sickness resurfaced. Mbuso camped outside Ma's room; Fikile laid a small mattress for him to sleep on.

On the fifth day, Ma woke up, made soft sour porridge and tea for everyone. A week later she announced she was going to look for a job. Fikile raised her eyebrows and pursed her lips, my sister had taken a certain tone of testiness with Ma, which left an uncomfortable taste in my mouth. Ma came back that afternoon holding a short-sleeved khaki shirt and black skirt. The shirt had a small sign, *Motherland Guest Lodge*, embroidered on the top left corner and *Housekeeping* printed in white at the back. She put on the uniform for us, and paraded around the living room. Mbuso and I *oohed* and *aahed* and clapped. Fikile looked up from the magazine on her lap for a second with that jaded expression of hers.

Ma said the job was temporary. She also said Mrs Hopkins was kind enough to provide a good reference.

"You show them that you can work hard, and that job will be yours permanently, sisi," Auntie Betty said.

Ma only wore the uniform for a month, she stopped working two months before her contract ended and spent her days in various stages of intoxication. On her third job in six months, things started to look as if they would change. For a few months Ma woke up every morning, prepared bread and tea for us, and walked to Doctor Thusi's surgery where she cleaned, washed towels and bed linen and made him tea and rusks. She spoke well of the doctor, of his gen-

128

tleness with the staff and patients. She even joked about how if she were still young and full of energy, she would go back to school to study nursing and come back to work with Doctor Thusi.

We came home from school one afternoon and found Ma sitting outside staring at the horizon, an empty bottle of liquor at her side. Mbuso was so elated at finding Ma home, he went and sat next to her and showed her his school report. Fikile passed her without uttering a word, went inside the house, changed from her school uniform and left. Ma called her name, Fikile marched on. I was so overwhelmed with the fear of my sister not returning that I started running after her. Mbuso stood and called my name. I kept running. I loved my sister to the point of tears. Fikile looked back and saw me. She stopped, told me not to be silly, that she was only going to her friend's house. Fikile did not come home until the early hours of the following morning. I had fallen asleep on the couch waiting for her. When I woke up, she was sitting next to me in her red-and-black dressing gown, drinking tea. She smiled and winked and asked if I wanted tea too.

Ma did not look for another job after that. We watched her world collapse and curve into itself like a sinkhole. We began to rely on each other, even Mbuso knew not to expect anything from Ma by then. When he came home one day from school, holding his shoes, seething with fury, his face streaked with dry tears, the soles having come undone while he was playing soccer at break, rendering him the school's laughing stock for the day, he went to Fikile.

Fikile said my job from then on was to care for our younger brother. I was to make sure he ate, washed, did his homework and did not come home from play too late. She said she would beat me into a pulp if anything bad ever happened to him. I did not fear my sister, but in that moment of her speaking to me in a hushed tone, I knew I would never want to be on her wrong side. I began to cry from the weight of the task. I wanted to scream that I did not ask to be my brother's keeper.

"Don't cry," Fikile said. "Of course I will not beat you, but I'm serious about you looking after your brother, okay? I want you to promise me that you will."

I promised.

Fikile merely tolerated Ma after that. The sour relationship between them only ended when Fikile started getting sick and Ma cleaned up her life and took over Fikile's.

* * *

Sizwe arrives early from work. He has washed and changed from his overalls into plain clothes but the smell of grease lingers. It is a smell I've grown accustomed to, look forward to at the end of each day. Mbuso puts his bottle of beer aside, stands, and shakes Sizwe's extended hand. This is the first time they are meeting. I watch the two men settle around me with measured comfort. Sizwe has heard Mbuso's name mentioned in many conversations with varying degrees of emotions – sweet nostalgia, irritation, accusation, sharp

embarrassment, hope. Mbuso knows little of the man standing next to me.

My friend Eunice joins us shortly after Sizwe. She ex-
changes a familiar hug with Sizwe and latches onto me
until I feel her warm tears on my shoulder. After a few
minutes, Eunice steps aside, wipes her eyes, and waits to
be introduced to my brother.

"It's Mbuso," I say.

"You said he was little," Eunice says extending her hand
towards Mbuso.

"Not anymore," I say. I feel my brother blushing next to
me.

"Welcome home. Try to stay put this time, okay? I know
those women in there drive this one crazy but they mean
well."

I met Eunice when I started my job at the municipality.
She was not easy to miss; her loud voice and belly laugh
that reverberated across the room belied her small frame
and delicate features. They called her Dynamite. Eunice had
been working there as a human resources administrator for
two years when I joined. Perhaps because we were closer
in age than the others, we had hit it off immediately and
haven't left each other's side.

We sit at our usual place at the back of the house forming
a circle. It could be an ordinary summer night, but it's not.
We take turns to talk about Fikile.

"I have always wondered if Fikile truly loved Thiza,"
Eunice says. "Beyond the allure of the teacher–student

affair. Beyond Thiza playing the saviour, the obvious exchange, Fikile's youth for money – though one could argue that the age gap between them wasn't so big, Thiza couldn't have been older than twenty-three, -four at the time – was there true love between them or was it a transaction, a sacrifice on her side? Would she have chosen him under normal circumstances had she not felt she needed his mercy?"

"Come on, it's obvious he took advantage of her. Let's call this what it was," Mbuso says firmly. "Fikile was a child and vulnerable, at sixteen what do you know about love? There are rules in life, teacher–student relationships should remain exactly that."

"I'm not disputing that at all. We can't also overlook the fact that the two went on to create a lifetime together, which is why I want to know from Anele: Did she love him, ever?" Eunice asks.

Everyone turns to me as if I'm the holder of Fikile's love vault.

"Yes, Fikile loved Thiza," I say. "It pains me to admit this given the dysfunctional state of their relationship, but damn, Fikile's love for that man was pure and relentless. There were events that tested and shook her to the core, left her heart torn in a million little pieces. I would listen as she spoke with a voice full of tremors and hurt, and think, this is it, she is finally going to leave. Fikile would go quiet for a few days, disappear, and then boom, with the clarity of a blue sky, she would announce coolly that they've patched things up, gathered the little pieces of her heart and neatly sewn them together. She made sure she left no room for discussion, for my protestations. She was swift and decisive, one of the qualities I hated and admired about her. So no, it was not just about the money, although we did need it at the time. There was love and loyalty underneath the chaos."

I don't tell them that at thirteen, I, too, loved Thiza. He was my hero. I had even prayed for him to take me as his wife instead of Fikile, make me scream his name the way my sister did when he visited our house in the middle of the night and snuck off with Fikile to our unfinished garage, certain we were all asleep.

"Still doesn't change the fact Thiza exploited her youth," Mbuso comments.

"Absolutely, he crossed the line, except you couldn't tell Fikile anything about Thiza," I say. "She was stubborn about him, tolerated so much of his shit."

"Too much shit," Eunice adds.

Fikile and Thiza fought. A lot. They fought over abundance of money, and when it dried, the lack of it. They fought over Thiza's intermittent states of amnesia that left him missing for days at a time, only to resurface without wanting to *talk about it*. The profile of women in my brother-in-law's life changed over the years, the schoolgirls replaced by mature women of Fikile's age, interested in neither his ragged car nor old fame. These were sistas Fikile worshipped with, members of her stokvel group, her children's teachers, nurses who treated her illness. They owned their homes, cars, paid for everything themselves. They struck up conversation with Fikile, friendships even, sent their children to her preschool and even helped her raise funds for a new playground and teaching aids. Fikile knew of their intentions, and yet, invited them in.

"Whatever happened to Thiza's ex-wife, what was her name?" Mbuso asks.

"Lindiwe, she left. I haven't seen her since, and I'm glad. I carried guilt about her and Thiza's breakup for the longest time. I felt I had personally contributed to the end of their dream."

"You didn't do anything," Eunice says. "Thiza was a cheat then, is a cheat now, and will always be one."

I tell them that Lindiwe did not accept her fate without a fight. Even before Fikile fell pregnant with Khanya, graduating from a schoolgirl to an instant family member, Lindiwe had tried to have a woman-to-woman talk with her. Fikile, in turn, taunted her with obvious cheekiness, the obstinacy of a hormonal girl. I was there when Lindiwe came to our house to speak to my sister. She arrived in her car and parked under the tree. An unexpected guest. I saw her first, and went inside to fetch Fikile who was ironing our school shirts to wear the following day.

"What does she want?"

"She says she wants to speak to you."

"I'm coming, don't let her in."

Fikile took her time to switch off the iron. As she stepped out, her face was impatient and sour. She stood by the door, arms tight across her chest, barely acknowledging Lindiwe's greetings, and said no to her request to come inside the house. My sister's behaviour was as if to display Lindiwe's desperation to the world. I sat in the lounge, pretending to be busy with homework.

Lindiwe spoke softly, devoid of threats and violence. "I came here to talk to you as an older sister, as someone who wants the best for you. I've known you for a while now, Fikile, you and your siblings. I know you're a smart girl with potential to break out of the cycle of poverty. You can go to university and make something of yourself, make your mother proud, wouldn't that be great? I can help you."

Fikile had mimicked Lindiwe to me afterwards, though we both knew I had listened to their entire conversation.

Lindiwe told Fikile she was not the first girl Thiza had an affair with, and would not be the last. "As a sister, I'm advising you to walk away from him before he ruins your future and you end up hurt. I know what I'm talking about, I've seen it happen to many girls before you. Most drop out of school, become packers at SaveMore Supermarket, while he continues to live his life. You don't want that, do you?"

Fikile did not speak, I knew she was soaking up every word, every expression to regurgitate, with added effects and theatrics, to her friends later. I pictured her pursing her thick lips and rolling her eyes at every instant.

"Thiza doesn't love you. I'm sorry I have to be the one to say this but it is the truth." Lindiwe sighed as if she had suddenly run out of breath. "Promise me you will consider what I've just said?"

As I sat there eavesdropping on my sister's conversation, I was overcome with the feeling of betrayal. I liked Lindiwe, she was beautiful and kind, and though I was never in her class, she sought me out. She sent me to run small errands for her and in return gave me fruits, snacks, and sometimes pressed silver coins into my hands. But even at my young age, I understood the improvement in our lives since Thiza came into the picture.

Lindiwe's goodbye was cheerful as if she was sensing victory. Many years later when I thought about that visit, I wondered if Lindiwe had resigned herself to the task of calling on her husband's mistresses and striking similar bargains. In the end, Lindiwe lost. When Fikile fell pregnant with Lesihle, four years after Khanya, Lindiwe woke up one morning, packed her suitcases, buckled her toddler daughter in the back seat and drove off. Divorce papers came to Thiza a few months later.

My sister never did get a white wedding, but Thiza paid full lobolo for her after his divorce became official. We accompanied them to the Home Affairs office the following year, and held a small celebration at home afterwards. Fikile poured her life into making a home for Thiza and her children.

*   *   *

Like a breeze, Thiza appears without warning and finds us congregated in his name. We jump at seeing him, exchange fleeting looks, each questioning how much he has heard.

"Thiza," I say moving towards him, and when I'm close enough, offer an embrace. Thiza's large frame swallows me, and we rock back and forth in this position for a minute. Unexpectedly Thiza's body starts to quiver, his anguish catches me unaware. My eyes turn to Eunice who is clutching her mouth to pacify her cries. I let Thiza cry on my shoulder until he calms down. I am embarrassed by my behaviour, dismissing Thiza as if he is incapable of pain, as if Fikile was only ours and he does not deserve to feel heartache for her.

Sizwe stands, his hug is brief and full of compassion. Mbuso offers his hand to his brother-in-law. The last time they saw each other, Mbuso was nineteen and mean. It takes a moment for Thiza to recognise him, and when he does, he pulls Mbuso to him and pours his heart out all over again. I stand a foot away, watching. I ask Thiza if he's been inside the house. He says no. We walk in together. There is silence when we enter, then a chorus of renewed grief and relief, the widower finally come to bid his wife farewell. I leave Thiza in his rightful place clutching his mother, and wailing like a bull.

*   *   *

Auntie Ntombi's car is brimming with groceries. She steps out, followed by her youngest child, my nephew Vuma, and

Khanya who trails behind, his head hanging low. Mvula and Bafana run to him, shouting, "Khanya! Khanya! What did you bring us?" Lesihle is sitting on the veranda steps, watching. Her body starts to quiver when she sees her brother. Khanya comes up to her, his arms outstretched, and takes her hand. They walk away from the house, out of the gate, without speaking. Bafana and Mvula stand by the gate calling their names and threatening to tell on them for going outside the yard at night. Khanya and Lesihle continue walking.

Auntie Ntombi is the baby of my mother's side of the family and the most educated, a high-school principal at a Model C school, glamorous, and distant, perhaps because of the age difference that exists among the three sisters – ten years between her and Ma, fourteen with Auntie Betty, the first born. My grandmother had fallen pregnant unexpectedly at an advanced age. After seven months of carrying the baby, her body had given up. The clinic nurses saved the child.

Auntie Ntombi lets out a loud, dramatic shriek as she enters the lounge, rattling the calm. She throws herself on the mattress at her older sister's feet, the aggrieved, the person she, Ntombi, once politely told was no longer welcome at her house, unless she cleaned herself up and became a respectable human being again.

"You understand why I'm saying this, Margaret?" Auntie Ntombi said back then. "It's not that we don't like having you in our home, we do. But you can't show up drunk and

138

with people we don't know. Do you know what Joseph said after you left, 'Your family is a disgrace.' That hurt me, sisi. His words hurt me very much. He had no right to speak that way about you or any member of my family, but as much as it pains me here," she pointed at her chest, "the man is telling the truth. Anele, you hear me, baby girl?"

I glared at my aunt, said nothing. I hated her for being so direct, for managing to keep an arm's length to Ma's problem and talking as if Ma could wake up one day and snap out of her alcoholism.

"Don't give me that look, Margaret, as if I'm being unreasonable. I'm speaking the truth." Auntie Ntombi's voice was accusing. Years as a principal dealing with discrimination, teen pregnancy, drugs, rape, hunger, toilet fights and stabbings, and graffiti had left her resilient and stony.

"But Ntombi, you know Mavuso?" Ma responded after some time as if she had been searching for her accomplice's name in her head. "He was a good friend to Meshack. You must remember him. He came to our house all the time."

"I don't know him," my aunt snapped. "And whether I know him or not is beside the point. You can't show up unannounced, sisi. What if we were not home? You would have travelled all the way for nothing."

"But you were home, weren't you? Our visit was not a waste," Ma said triumphant.

Auntie Ntombi's nostrils flared. She opened her mouth and closed it, aware she would not win. She smiled at Ma, then said to no one in particular, "Do we have any ripe mangoes? I've been craving them lately and you know I don't even like them. If I wasn't my age I would think I'm pregnant." She paused, laughed. As she was leaving, she turned to me with a stern face, as if I was part of the naughty visiting gang. "Watch where she goes, would you? I don't want to have to deal with this again."

* * *

A surprise visit to Auntie Ntombi's house was the reason she later forbade Ma to set foot there. Ma brought with her an old friend, Baba Mavuso, who, according to my aunt, launched into a snoring slumber as soon as he sat down, that even Ma's hard jabs couldn't break. Auntie Ntombi called Fikile to fetch the intruding visitors. Fikile, with only a learner's licence, picked me up and drove us the hour to our aunt's house.

"Your uncle is traumatised by this experience," Ntombi said, leading Fikile and I inside. "He has never seen your mother like this. You should have seen them, it was like a circus had come to camp at my house. Why did she come here, and with him?"

"She came here because you are her sister, where else must she go?" Fikile barked.

We found Ma and Baba Mavuso slumped on the sofa, mouths hanging open and lines of saliva flowing down their cheeks. Fikile was convinced the reason Auntie Ntombi had not loaded them in her car and taken them home herself, was to show us the *evidence*, so that we would not later roll

140

our eyes when she related the story and accuse her of exaggerating. Fikile and I each hooked our arms around Baba Mavuso and lifted him. He slid off the couch without protest, without so much as a word. Fikile guided him towards the car.

Ma balked. "Why are you taking me away from my sister? You didn't bring me here, I came on my own, I'll leave when I'm ready. Get your dirty hands off me, you child. I can walk by myself. Anele, why are you doing this to your mother? Ntombi, tell them to leave me alone."

"They are taking you home, Margaret, it's late. You need some sleep."

"But I came here to see you."

"I know, and now it's time to go. Let the kids take you home."

"I see. You don't want me. You don't want me in your house. Fine, I'll go and never come back. We will never set foot here again, not me, not my children, not my children's children." She spat and walked away, still mumbling angrily for us to follow her.

As I was opening the car door, I heard Auntie Ntombi mutter under her breath, "Why did God take Meshack and leave this one?" I slammed the door so hard I startled everyone.

"Why did you go there and make a fool of yourself, Ma?" Fikile's words flew out as soon as she pulled out of Auntie Ntombi's driveway. Ma, seated at the back, staring out of the window at the disappearing suburban streetlights, said nothing. "You know how Ntombi is, what she thinks of you. She does not care for you, Ma. Get that in your head. You embarrass her. We embarrass her. Promise me you will never go to her house on your own."

"Ntombi is my sister. I will visit her whenever I want."

"She doesn't want you, Ma!"

"Ma, Fikile is right. And you also know this."

Ma's sobs were expected; any situation hinting at a confrontation elicited such an outpour. "Nobody loves me. You all pretend that you do, but I know deep in your hearts you wish me dead. I am an irritation to you. You think I don't know this? You're wrong, I know. That I'm a drunkard does not mean I am blind. Even Betty, she is pretending. I know what she says behind my back, then she comes to my house and drinks tea with me and pretends she cares. She is bitter from her solitude and childlessness because I chased that man away. Betty was always jealous of me, even as children, she always found ways to make me feel inadequate. I never said anything but showed her kindness and respect as my older sister. At least Ntombi hates me to my face. And then my son, my own son deserted me, and my daughters, who should be caring for me in my old age, are waiting for the moment I stop breathing so they can celebrate."

"Ma, stop," I said.

"Stop what? You think I don't know that you want my husband's house, the house he built with his own sweat? Why have you not married and moved to your own house? Why are you still lingering around, bossing me like a child,

142

Ma do this, don't do that? Why have you brought a man inside your father's house? What do you think people are saying? You think I don't know the game you're playing? You and Sizwe think you will take over the house when I die? Never. Over my dead body! And you, Fikile, I can only feel sorry for you for marrying that *nonsonso* of a man. You've chosen a horrible life, my child. I have tried to rescue you, but you keep going back to that misery. I cannot help you now. As for your brother, that little ungrateful bastard, he can go to hell. I sacrificed for him so he can get education and become a better man. And how does he thank me? By pretending I don't exist. His own mother. Anyway, I don't care about him; he is not my child anymore, he is as good as dead to me. The only person who ever loved me is long dead. Can I tell you something? I also want to die. I can't take this anymore."

I remember many things about Baba. I remember how he loved Ma. When he was home and in a jovial mood, sometimes from having one too many beers at Uncle So-and-so's house, or after winning a few hundred rands from *fafi*, Baba would tell us a story of a farm girl who came to New Hope as part of a bridal party and never left. Baba had made his intentions clear from day one of meeting Ma, young and shy and the most beautiful woman New Hope had ever seen, not even the new bride could compare. He wasted no time sending his delegates to start the lobolo negotiation. He was a bachelor, a *catch,* with a good job. Him choosing Ma, a stranger, disappointed the ladies of New Hope who had their sights on him. Baba related this story many times, yet each time he told it, it was as if for the first time. A spark would fly between them, leaving both flushed with affection, such that Ma would put aside whatever irritation we had imposed on her and take my father's extended hand and dance with him, much to our delight. On Sunday afternoons, after we had returned from church and eaten lunch, Baba and Ma would sit on the veranda facing the street and greet neighbours passing by.

"Are you done?" Fikile asked Ma with a tone of mild amusement.

"I want to die."

"Do us all a favour and stop going over to that woman's house uninvited. That's all we are asking from you."

Fikile continued driving; we had gone through this before, many times. The ending was always the same – Ma waking up before everyone else the next morning, waiting for me in the kitchen, her face clouded in embarrassment, the gnawing thought of having been inappropriate, yet never quite recalling the detail, the extent of the damage. The misunderstandings between us settled over tea and sweet, buttery soft porridge, made the way I like it. New commitments entered, the possibility of rehabilitation suggested by Ma herself, and familiar peace maintained. And life would go on.

"Ma is right about Sizwe and me," I said before Fikile drove off.

"Don't be silly. Sizwe is the best thing to happen to us."

"But she is right about him living with us, this is not the way it's supposed to be. Maybe we should move out."

"Anele, Ma has said the most atrocious things to me. She has called me every name under the sun since I was sixteen, do you think if I took everything she says to heart I would still be talking to her? Don't listen to her. You're not doing anything wrong." She was quiet for a second, then added, "You can't leave Ma alone, not now, she will fall apart."

"I can't stay with her forever either. Ma will not get better, we both know that."

"Let's just give it time."

"Ma doesn't want to get better, Fikile."

"Please, Anele."

"I'm out of here next year, whether she stops drinking or not. I'm out."

My sister looked at me long and said, "This is really bothering you?"

I nodded.

She came around to where I was standing, pulled me to her. "I'm sorry, I didn't know."

"Am I a bad person for wanting to abandon my mother like this?"

"No, you're not."

*　*　*

Auntie Betty and Uncle Majaha took Ma to the government rehabilitation centre two hundred kilometres away from our

145

town. My father had been dead for two years. A few days before they left, Auntie Betty sat us down, explained the trouble Ma was in. Mbuso, glued to Ma's lap, looked at my aunt with wet eyes. Auntie Betty suggested moving in with us until Ma was back. Fikile declined the gesture, saying she could look after us. She and Thiza had started dating.

Ma was gone for two months. She left with a small, checked suitcase, and bewilderment. She came back looking like the person she once was. She woke up early the next morning to see us off to school. She cleaned the house, took down curtains and washed them, moved furniture, scraped the Hart pots until years of stubborn scorching came off and the enamel sparkled. On days when she wasn't cleaning the house or mending old clothes, Ma went out to look for work. On those days, she wore her favourite brown, wool two-piece skirt suit and a cream white shirt, tucked in. She came back each afternoon without a job but her dignity remained intact.

The second time at rehab, a couple of years after the first stint, she lasted two weeks before she called Auntie Betty to fetch her. She came home and went straight to bed. Rehabilitation was never discussed again in our family except in Ma's moments of disgrace but we all knew she did not mean it.

* * *

When Auntie Ntombi is done emptying her melancholy at Ma's feet, she lifts herself to a sitting position on the mattress and rearranges her doek, which has come undone. She says to me, "Tell me, did Sizwe buy a new car? Are things going that well for him?"

Auntie Betty snorts as if Ntombi has cracked a joke. "Please, don't mock Sizwe. Where do you think a simple handyman like him would get money to buy a big machine like that? Did you see *that thing* properly? It's a house."

"It's Mbuso's car," Ma says.

My aunt's eyes dilate; she looks up at me, incredulous. "Your brother is here?"

"My boy arrived this afternoon, praise be to God. I never thought I would see him again."

"*Jesu*! The earth has opened up and spit out our son." She claps her hands. "Fikile had to die for him to remember home. Bring him here. That boy's nerve!"

*   *   *

"I won't be here for you forever," Fikile once said. I was in grade seven, and had just turned thirteen. My sister was nearly seventeen. Fikile came home with two plastic bags full of groceries – a block of margarine, soft and folded at the edges, a tin of apricot jam, Mbuso's favourite, cooking oil, sugar, dry soup, crunchy peanut butter and baked beans – food we had not tasted in months. She dumped the groceries on the kitchen table with such force I feared she had broken the peanut butter bottle.

Fikile glared at Mbuso and me. "You hear me? I said I will not be here to feed you forever. I'm not your mother. I'm not

147

your father. I didn't bring you into this world, I'm not responsible for you and I cannot be expected to raise you. I have my own life to live." She dragged out "own life" as if she wanted the words to stay engraved in our minds.

Mbuso who was chanting "What did you bring us, sisi? What did you bring us, sisi?" recoiled, and came to stand by me, eyes glassy and lips trembling.

I remained glued to the spot between the table and the stove with my sweaty forehead and the wooden spoon laden with scraps of wet porridge in one hand. I had taken over the role of cooking when Fikile wasn't home. I knew not to speak to my sister when she was in her bad moods, which was becoming common and frankly – I reasoned – unfair to us.

Fikile was not wearing her school uniform; it was not the first time she returned from school in her "home" clothes. I knew the uniform was folded neatly and tucked inside her school bag, together with a Ziploc bag containing vanishing cream that made her skin look smooth and powdery like a ghost, thick black eyeliner, a lipstick – lollipop pink or red like a Coca-Cola can – deodorant spray, a face cloth, and a bar of coconut-smelling soap. Ma was not aware of this or what Fikile and I got up to behind the boulders to pass time and fantasise about a life elsewhere. Ma had not read Mbuso's school reports, with skewed stars and remarks – *EXCELLENT, CLEVER BOY, A BRIGHT STAR* – scribbled all over. Ma was blind to most of the happenings around our house, our lives.

Fikile turned her back and walked to her room, slamming the door shut. A piece of concrete peeled from the wall and fell on the floor. Mbuso jumped with fright.

"Why is sisi angry at us?" Mbuso asked. We were packing away the groceries my sister had brought.

"She is not angry at us," I said to my brother. "Maybe one of her friends made her angry."

My sister leaving us was my worst fear. Sometimes I woke up in the middle of the night and tiptoed to Fikile's room, and cried when I found her bed empty. On those nights, which became frequent as the year wore on and the scandalous rumour spread of her relationship with one of her teachers, Sir Thokozani "Thiza" Dlamini, I did not go back to sleep until I heard the kitchen door lock turn and feet shuffle softly towards the end of the passage.

Fikile was four months pregnant with her first child, Khanya, when she finally confided in me. But I already knew – the morning fervent rush to the toilet followed by loud gagging; her unpredictable behaviour, dissolving into tears at the slightest provocation, like when Mbuso told her she was looking *big*, like almost fat but *not quite* fat; her sudden craving for chalk, clay, crumbling soil on the branches of our neighbour's hedge – things I had learned in my Biology class. I knew Fikile was *sleeping* and now she was pregnant. I was conflicted and disappointed, surely my sister was smarter and should have known to go to the clinic and get an injection to *prevent*. I never got to ask her why she didn't let Thiza empty his juices on her thighs instead.

Everyone who was *sleeping* knew the trick to not falling pregnant.

Fikile was calm as she told me that she would leave school, enrol at the night school to complete her matric; she was adamant that she was going to write her final exams. She said she would raise the child on her own if she had to, because as things were, Thiza was acting *funny*, as if he was not part of the life growing inside her. She let me touch her swollen stomach, which was smooth and hard, a well-defined roundness.

"What are you going to tell Ma?" I asked, though I knew that in Fikile's view, our mother had ceased to exist and therefore her opinions did not matter.

"I'm not telling her anything. You're not telling her anything either."

By the seventh month, clever layers of oversized clothes could not hide Fikile's pregnancy, and the rumours of her being with child circulated widely at our school, in turn rendering my life a living hell like I was the one who was sleeping with the teacher. I was certain everyone was talking about my sister, as if she was the first person in our township to fall pregnant, and by a teacher. My friends avoided me for a while, perhaps they thought my sister's pregnancy would rub off on them. I kept to myself, went straight home after school, did my homework and played with my brother, who was oblivious to the happenings around him. Only months later, after Khanya arrived, did one of the girls on my street confess that her parents had forbidden her from hanging out with me. She said her mother said Fikile and I were nothing but trouble.

Fikile remained unscathed by the gossip and stares, but she did drop out and, with Auntie Betty's help, enrolled at a school that allowed her to attend classes at night and write exams. When Ma eventually found out about the pregnancy, much later than anyone else, and only because Auntie Betty told her, she threw a drunken fit and chased Fikile out of her house.

"I will not share my house with another woman," Ma screamed, and started pulling Fikile's clothes out of her closet, throwing them into a pile outside the kitchen door. "You're a woman now, Fikile, right? You know how to open your legs for a man? Well, go and be a woman in your own house, not here. I'm raising children here."

Ma turned to me. "And you," she said, wriggling her shaking finger, "if you ever bring such shame on my house you know what will happen to you."

Ma's words were as sharp as a blade and cut through my heart. I had done nothing to deserve her explosion. Had I not been a good girl who never strayed, obedient to the house rules? Had I not watched over Mbuso, brought only good grades home, cooked when Fikile was out until the early hours of the morning? Had I not helped Ma out of her clothes when she was too drunk to undress herself, brought her strong black coffee in the morning to nurse her hangover before rushing off to school?

Fikile collected her clothes and put them in small plastic

bags, and took a taxi to Auntie Betty's house. Mbuso and I walked with her to the main road.

"You must both go to school, okay?" Fikile said before boarding the taxi. "I'll be back soon."

Mbuso waved until the taxi disappeared, and then he cried. When we returned home, Ma had locked the gates. We spent the night at Auntie Maria's house. I was so hurt, I did not speak to my mother for several days. I don't think she even noticed.

the truth about bafana

Uncle Majaha is the first person from my paternal side to make an appearance, to show his solidarity with his brother's widow. He left the mines early in the morning, stopping only once for tea and a restroom break, he tells the women – Ma, her two sisters, Thiza's mother, and Auntie Maria – who have regrouped in Fikile's lounge. He says he ingratiated himself with the foreman, who let him go a few days before the mine closed for the festive season. Uncle Majaha rubs his eyes and brings his hands to his mouth, uttering Fikile's name as Ma relates to him her daughter's last days. Ma has that look of utter weariness and downheartedness; I feel a surge of sadness for her.

"Death is a thief," Uncle Majaha says when Ma stops talking, his words full of regret. "We travelled many roads with this child. I'm old but I learned a lot from umafungwase." My uncle referred to Fikile as the first born, I've only heard him call her name once, when she refused to name Thiza as the father of her first child.

I now know it was not an accident that Fikile fell pregnant. I know that she did it for us. I also know that Thiza had threatened her to get rid of the child, and when she wouldn't, begged her not to point to him as the father for fear of losing his job. He made her believe that everyone, including us, would lose if she told the truth. Then he promised to continue supporting her, and even marry her once the matter with Lindiwe was finalised. Fikile agreed. When Uncle Majaha wanted to set a date to pay Thiza a visit to report the damages, Fikile objected. Uncle Majaha wasn't convinced by her protest, he called the whole thing disrespectful to his dead brother, their family name, and dragged Fikile to the Dlaminis to put an end to the shame.

Uncle Majaha was right, Thiza was under no threat to lose his job. That he had love affairs with his students was common knowledge. It was also common knowledge that the residents of our location didn't bat an eyelid about these affairs. Only when the girl got herself knocked-up and chucked out of school – this after the layers of oversized sweaters could not conceal the protruding belly – did the they look up and murmur, their voices condemning the promiscuous girl. Even then they merely shrugged at the teacher. Thiza had successfully denied two pregnancies before Fikile's.

Uncle Majaha and Auntie Betty went to Thiza's family to inform them of Fikile's pregnancy. Thiza denied responsibility outright, said he was an honourable man, a dedicated teacher and that he would not do such a thing to a child in his care. Besides, he was happily married, the entire township had witnessed his union. Why would he risk his marriage over schoolgirls? The delegates left, their heads hanging in shame, because of the embarrassment their daughter had caused. Thiza stopped coming to our house.

Khanya was born two months later with the brightest set of eyes as if to light up the world, true to his name.

Everyone cooed and loved him, even Ma, who we found waiting at Auntie Betty's the day Fikile was discharged from the hospital. Hands shaking and reeking of beer, Ma lifted the barely two-day-old baby, Auntie Betty hawk-eyed right beside her, whispering, "Don't drop the baby now, Margaret. Don't drop the baby." There was such ease in the way Ma handled the baby, like she and Khanya had met before and this was merely a show for everybody else. A month later Fikile moved back home from Auntie Betty's where she had been staying.

Ma did not take Thiza's rejection lying down; she talked to anyone who cared to listen about his cowardice, how he ruined her child and lacked the civility to own up to his filth. Thiza's mother eventually got wind of the story. She showed up at our house one Saturday morning to see the child, took one look at Khanya and cried out, "Idlozi! He is a spitting image of Madlihlathi, Thiza's late great-grandfather. I can spot that forehead anywhere." She lifted the screaming infant, held him up like she was about to make a sacrifice and started chanting the Dlamini clan names to Ma's delight. That laid the matter of Khanya's paternity to rest. The Dlaminis welcomed Khanya to their family. A boy. Fikile, a girl of nineteen, had blessed them with a gift that their son's wife of three years had dismally, and quite embarrassingly for the family, failed to. A few weeks later, Thiza came to apologise. Ma told him to *fokof*.

Uncle Majaha is a constant in our lives. After my father died, he assumed the task of checking on us. Once or twice a year when he was home on leave, he brought food in large quantities – bags of maize and rice, dried beans, vegetable oil, and meat and bones. He left white envelopes with Ma, and later with Fikile, remembered our birthdays – sent cards that sang when opened and dropped ten, twenty, and fifty rand notes.

"Your brother would have been proud of you," Ma would say blinking back tears, after receiving another act of kindness from her brother-in-law.

Uncle Majaha celebrated our achievements, and once told us to pack our bags and loaded everyone in his double cab and drove for several hours through the night. We woke up to the glistening bluish-grey waters at a distance. We screamed as the car approached the sea and we could smell the pungent, unfamiliar smell, see the waves crashing furiously, one after the other, on the shore.

Uncle Majaha not only delivered a heavily pregnant Fikile to the Dlaminis, but also presided over her lobolo negotiations.

Fikile's house is quiet for a while. Ma wipes her nose. I feel a prickle form at the back of my eyes.

Suddenly Auntie Ntombi feigns surprise that Uncle Majaha has not brought in the extra help of a *small house* to assist during the funeral. "You know very well that some of us don't have the energy to peel and cook and carry tea and scones all day."

Uncle Majaha bursts out laughing as if it's the best joke

he's heard in a long time, we all join in. The love I suddenly feel for my aunt swells in my heart, I want to hug her, tell her I love her with all her faults.

"Unfortunately small houses are expensive to maintain, Ntombi. I cannot keep up with their demands," Uncle Majaha responds, his voice still full of laughter. "I'm an old man too, can't you see my head is as grey as the clouds? I need a grown woman."

Uncle Majaha's wife, Gcinile, died a few years back after a long battle with diabetes, leaving him with two adult children who have since left home. My uncle never married again, although in the early months of his wife's passing, rumours surfaced and circulated widely about him taking on another wife. Uncle Majaha only laughed and said people should keep to their own business. Then one December he arrived with a red seshweshwe- and doek-wearing brunette named Yvette, whom he introduced to the family as his *good* friend and made us children call her Auntie Yvette. Ma had invited my uncle and his girlfriend for lunch that Sunday. She made us take our baths and put on our best clothes, she said if there was one person in the world worth all the effort it was our uncle. She stayed sober for two whole days.

Auntie Betty came to our house early that morning and helped Ma cook up a storm of rice, chicken stew, and a colourful array of salads and vegetables. Uncle Majaha and his girlfriend arrived to a house filled with rich aromas and shiny-faced children. We all received gifts from the couple – chocolates and money which Uncle Majaha shoved into our hands under the cover of a discreet handshake. We – Fikile, Mbuso and I – were so giddy with joy we declared that day our best ever and prayed for Auntie Yvette to marry our uncle. I can't recall what happened to Yvette. She did not return the following holidays and that was the end of that story.

"Now you are talking, s'bali, I support that thought. And you know the saying, 'Sometimes what you're looking for is right under your nose and you don't even know it'." Auntie Betty throws a glance in my direction, and winks. We both turn to Auntie Maria, who is looking down, besieged by shyness.

My uncle laughs again, but with tenderness, and asks my aunt when did she become a matchmaker.

"Tell your brother to come greet your uncle," Ma whispers to me.

* * *

My cell phone rings nonstop. I am patient with the callers, accept their condolences and offers of support – what can they do, what can they bring? How are the children doing? And Thiza, widowed at such a young age, how will he cope with three children? And finally Ma, how is she, that poor woman, hasn't she just been through a lot in this life? I allow each one to recount fond memories of my sister, share tears followed by abrupt apologetic utterances, "Please forgive me, Anele, I'm selfish, you've lost a sister, you should be crying to me!" I listen until the sentiments run dry, and the

160

conversation moves to the pragmatic, the logistics of the day before the burial, the memorial service, and the burial day itself. With times confirmed and promises of seeing each other on such-and-such a day affirmed, I hang up, only to take another call a few minutes later.

I do not recognise the number flashing on my screen.

"Hello, is that Anele Mabuza?" It is an unfamiliar voice on the other side of the line.

"Yes," I respond. My voice is now trained to remain amiable to strangers.

"My name is Sello Mabe. I knew your sister."

It is a familiar name, long buried in my memory. My heart skips. Sello Mabe, a man from Fikile's past. "I know who you are."

"I am sorry about your sister."

"Thank you."

I step out of the kitchen and move towards the garage, a safe place from the commanding voices: "Has everyone eaten? Mbuso, my son, do you want another cup of tea, bread? Where is Khanya? Taking a nap? A nap for what, wake him up, there is no time for sleep."

"Why can't he sleep, Gogo? It's not like we have somewhere to go."

"Lesihle, stop asking questions and go wake your brother!"

I wait for Sello to speak, and when he doesn't, I fill the silence. "The funeral is on Saturday morning if you would like to come, we will start at seven. I can send you the church's address, it will be easier if you go straight there."

"I'm afraid I will not be able to come." He speaks with the strained voice of someone warding off tears. He requests to meet, in town, in an hour. "Can you make it?"

"You are here?"

"I'll be in town in half an hour. I'm sorry I'm asking you now without notice. I didn't trust myself to go through with the drive. Your sister's passing has left me shaken."

"I don't know if it will be possible, we have people here, I have work to do in preparation –"

"Anele, it is important I speak to you today. I'm worried I may not have another chance," he says quietly, pleading.

I agree to meet Sello at The Willows Lodge – his suggestion. He gives me directions to the lodge, insists I call him if I get lost. "Not an easy place to find, almost on the outskirts of town," he adds.

In the end it is not difficult to escape the mayhem of relatives, friends, strangers, who have descended on Fikile's house. With Ma shedding buckets of tears on the mattress with each mourner coming to pay their respects, Auntie Betty instructing Uncle Majaha and Mbuso on the type of goat breed to purchase for the ceremony a night before the burial – "Don't take the boar, it will stink up the house, and the meat is tough" – and Auntie Ntombi supervising the baking in the kitchen – "We need more bicarbonate of soda, otherwise the scones won't taste nice. Who can go to the shops?" – I find the right moment to escape.

"I'll go," I volunteer, and decline Lesihle's offer to accompany me. "We will go shopping with your uncle tomorrow."

Lesihle purses her lips together and watches me like I might change my mind, I pretend not to see her. I grab my bag and car keys and leave in a shower of requests for this and that item.

The Willows Lodge is on the edge of town on a private farm overlooking a small stream as Sello described. Only when I enter the narrow road lined with giant willow trees do I realise I've been here before – the day of Fikile's breast prosthetic and mastectomy bra fitting and to celebrate the news of my pregnancy. I understand why this place was dear to my sister and why, until that lunch here with her, she had kept it a secret from me.

I enter the restaurant, and before I can scan the space for someone who could be Sello, the waiter approaches me, asks if I'm Anele, and shows me to a table occupied by a tall, broad-shouldered man with peppered hair in a white shirt and grey pants. He is talking quietly on his phone. The real Sello Mabe is not the Sello Mabe of my imagination, not a pot-bellied businessman with a penchant for flaunting his newfound wealth. There is no sloppiness about him, no sense of overbearing. He appears in control of his life, the type of allure that would appeal to Fikile. And, of course, he is the man in one of Fikile's photographs I found in the brown box in her closet.

"What does he look like?" I demanded to know when Fikile first spoke Sello's name. "What was he like?"

My sister had not immediately confessed the affair. I wonder if she would have, had the cancer not invaded her body and rearranged her life. It was shortly after her first chemo-therapy; she was weak and on bed rest when she first men-tioned Sello to me. She smiled to herself as she narrated her secret rendezvous with him.

"Like a man." Fikile laughed. "Life is not as straightfor-ward, does not follow some kind of clever numbering sys-tem. Sometimes you find yourself in situations you never dreamt of. I love my husband, you know that, but some-times you need someone to talk to, share ideas, dreams with, laugh with. And sometimes that person is not the one you're officially with," Fikile paused, appraised the look in my eyes. "It's difficult to explain. Sello is different to Thiza, worlds apart, not that I had intentionally sought to pit them against each other, they just are that different. Sello engages. He listens. He knows about things. He is a kind man and made me feel happiness all the way to the tips of my toes and fingers." She threw her head back and groaned with delight. "I love him."

"Love him? I thought –"

"I will always love him."

The affair had started at a time when Fikile was recon-structing the pieces of her life and was on a mission to free herself from Thiza's claws. Sello was somebody's relative in Fikile's early childhood development training group; a businessman who took delight in showing the relative and her two friends around town. He introduced them to places they didn't know existed, unusual cuisine, theatres, apart-heid museums, and left them charmed and delirious with city lights and high life. After the third outing with the group, Sello asked Fikile out to dinner, just the two of them. Fikile stalled, it wasn't right, they were both married. Sello did not ask her out again.

"He was sensitive in that regard, didn't want to make me feel uncomfortable. I admired that about him. He was a perfect gentleman."

They kept in touch. He called sometimes, followed up on progress at Fikile's crèche, small at the time and accommodating no more than fifteen children, the money enough to keep food on the table, clothes on their bodies and the lights on. He listened with sympathy when she complained about the incomplete set of chairs for the children, cracked chalkboard, the leaking roof, and insufficient toys and how the children fought over them. Each time Sello offered to help, Fikile turned him down, "I will make a plan, somehow. Life has a way of resolving its problems."

One day a truck pulled up outside Fikile's house loaded with school supplies – toys, charts, stationery, flash cards, books and bookshelves, a brand new whiteboard. There was also a note signed, *Please accept these items as my contribution to the education of our children. SM.* Fikile had cried.

Another time, weeks after furnishing the crèche, Sello called again, saying he was coming our town's way, could they meet in town for tea and catch up? They met several times at The Willows Lodge. Two years later, Fikile put an end to the affair and spent months in a miserable funk.

In hindsight, I recall the time of Sello's presence as one

of the happiest in my sister's life, though I had naively attributed the happiness to her newfound purpose.

My sister told me of Sello's thoughtfulness. He was a generous lover who constantly praised her and showered her with unexpected gifts – an oil heater to keep the children warm, a computer, which prompted Thiza to comment, "This business is making you money, and you're not even a proper teacher", expensive perfumes. In the years to come, long after the affair ended, Fikile always went back to that moment, frozen in her happiness archives. She told me that she wondered what would have happened had she left Thiza and pursued a full relationship with Sello.

"Why didn't you?"

"Sello is a married man, and I have travelled that journey before. It was complicated this time; I wasn't a teenager driven by recklessness and no cares. A lot was at stake for both of us. Anyway, all of that is in the past now."

As Fikile's condition improved and worsened once more, Sello Mabe never came up in our conversations again. I forgot he existed, until now.

Sello ends his chat and puts the phone away when he sees me. He stands and introduces himself, taking my hand in his. His grip is firm.

"I'm glad to finally meet you, Anele," Sello says, still holding onto my hand. "You are as beautiful as your sister described you. Please sit."

We chat briefly about the beauty of the place, his favourite in town, if not the country. "I know the owners, good people. You must come sometime when you need to breathe and forget the world for a moment."

I smile. This lovely man, my sister's lover, does not know it will cost me a day's work to even drink tea here. "I will consider it."

Sello orders lunch for us, salad and medium-rare steak for him and grilled fish, potato wedges and vegetables for me.

"How are you feeling?" Sello asks.

"Like I'm walking through thick fog, I can see what's in front of me but the horizon is a giant white wall."

"I know how close you were to your sister. I can't imagine what you're going through. I'm sorry for your loss, Fikile was a special person to me." He looks straight at me as he says this. "After all this time, I still think about her. Did she ever say anything about me?"

"She did."

"I'm glad," he smiles, satisfied. "Your sister was the most wonderful being, modest, caring, I wish I could have known her a little longer and spent more time with her. I often say it's all in the timing. Ours was mismatched from the beginning, the universe pulled us together, but it also made it complex for us to stay together. What do you call that?"

Sello leans back on his chair, retells his version of how they met, talks about his business interests, the four-star Mabe Boutique Hotels and Spas, a new one just opened on the coast, the expansion planned for other African countries, starting with Mozambique.

He watches me for a minute, smiles and says, "There is a

fire that lives within Africa and its people. You may break our bones, take away our possessions, dehumanise us, but the fire will continue to burn until all that is rightfully ours is restored."

Sello talks about his life in general – his three kids, his love for golf, and dream of designing and owning a golf course one day. He laughs to himself, "Not too shabby for a mine boy who started as a porter at one of the hotels." He does not mention his wife, and I don't ask. His face turns serious when he mentions my sister. "I loved your sister in every possible way; she was easy to love. During our time together, she gave me the universe. I never stopped loving her, thinking of her. Even now I wake up sometimes and see her. I remember everything, how she smelled, her shyness each time we saw each other, gradually unwinding into something beautiful that only two people with genuine fondness for each other can create. Fikile overturned everything I held true about who I am and what I stand for, what I thought I knew about love. I'll tell you that I have no regrets about our time together. I was a happy man."

I give Sello time to mourn Fikile, time to relive their lives.

"She adored you, Anele, would have moved the world for you. She loved your mother too, but admitted that she was not as close to her. And your brother, he was forever little and dear to her."

Sello tells me about their last moment together. "They say men don't cry, that's bullshit. I cried the day she told me she couldn't see me anymore. I knew the day would come when she would leave me, I was never prepared for the blows, the sharp jabs right to the centre of my heart, the reality of her words. Maybe I was in denial. Maybe I believed the impossible. Maybe I was becoming greedy, expected too much, and yet I knew she couldn't give all of herself."

"She was devastated too," I comment.

"It was a difficult time for both of us," he says.

We sit quietly for a while.

"I know you tried everything you could to save her, sought out the best treatments. The universe had other plans."

I think about how diligent Fikile was with her medications, how she never missed her chemotherapy and radiation treatments. She ate well, took her vitamins and short walks along our street, and yet she died.

"What can we say, death is a given for all of us, our destination. It is only a matter of time before we all succumb," Sello says.

"You –" I pause, reconstruct the sentence in my head. "I didn't know you kept in touch. Last time she spoke of you was four, five years ago. I had forgotten about you."

"We never lost touch." For the first time, Sello lets his guard down, his lower lip trembles as he fights to compose himself. He apologises, fishes out a grey handkerchief from his shirt pocket. He takes off his glasses and wipes his eyes, nose. I turn my face to the pool where a couple is lying on the pool chairs, their backs red from the sun. "I'm going through a challenging period in my life right now,

169

I've lost someone I loved dearly. Your sister was special to me."

"I'm sorry."

The waiter brings our food, heaped plates that we both know will be hardly touched. The owner saunters to our table, gentle smile on his face. Greetings are passed, introductions made, and promises made to catch up properly at some time.

"I suppose we must eat before the food gets cold, we don't want to offend the chef now," Sello says.

I take a few bites of my fish, and pick up a potato wedge chip and swirl it in the piri-piri sauce for a while, bite off a piece and try to swallow. It lodges in my throat; I take a sip of water to push it down. Finishing the meal will be a challenge.

Sello also struggles with his steak. He laughs. "Food was a bad idea." He sets the plate aside, beckons the waiter for a coffee refill. "There is something I need to talk to you about. How is Bafana?"

I imagine Fikile shared a lot of stories with Sello about her youngest child, born not too long after their affair. "He is a delightful little boy, charming, always cracking jokes, often unintentional, of course. He keeps us going, he understands what is going on, that his mother is gone to heaven and will never return to play with him or make him toast and jam, and warm milk."

"Will you let me know if there's anything I can do to make things better for you, for Bafana?"

I nod. "Thank you."

"Did Fikile say anything else about Bafana?"

"Like what?"

"The truth about Bafana's paternity?"

"Bafana is Thiza's child." I shift my weight, look straight at Sello.

"Bafana is a Mabe. Bafana is my son." Sello utters these words without blinking, without hesitation. He speaks with confidence, his voice so controlled as if to leave no room for me to doubt him.

"Bafana is Thiza's child," I say again not taking my eyes off him.

Sello shakes his head slowly, certainly.

I stare blankly at Sello, say nothing.

"When Fikile found out she was expecting our child, she ended our relationship. I pleaded with her for us to come clean, I was ready to take whatever journey lay ahead for us, with her by my side. She wouldn't hear of it. I loved her so much I respected her wishes. When Bafana was a year old, Fikile formally introduced us." He pauses, looks around with fondness. "We came here, spent the day together. We chased butterflies, searched for frogs, made a mud house by the riverbank, and ate lunch under the big willow tree by the river. A magical time. I saw Bafana again twice the following year, and a year after, and that was the end of our time here. Fikile wouldn't risk bringing him to me in case, as she put it: 'He told of his adventures by the river'. That was also the last time I saw him in the flesh. Over the years Fikile sent photographs – his fourth birthday, first day of grade R, and recently, last year, Bafana striking a pose in his brand-new clothes at a rap concert."

I find myself smiling. I know the picture Sello is referring to, Bafana in his famous hip-hop pose. Khanya had taken him and the girls to the concert by his *bestest* rap artist. For days afterwards, Bafana woke up rhyming to the songs.

"We revisited the conversation after Fikile became sick, she asked for time to focus on her health, a fair request. We agreed once she got better we would sit everyone down – my family, your family – and tell the truth. Never happened. Your sister got better as you're aware, but she said she wasn't ready. It seemed cruel for me to push the matter with Bafana. I thought we had time, I was wrong."

Sello stops talking, looks at me as if willing me to say something. When I do not speak, he sighs, leans back on the chair, the lethargy of confession visible in his eyes. "You must be angry at me for unloading my problems on you at a time when you're dealing with your sister's death. I know you have a million things to fix before the funeral. You must think I'm a selfish man."

It is only now that I think to ask how he heard about Fikile's death. "Nikiwe, my cousin who introduced us, called me with the news."

A day or two after Fikile died, I went through her phone, picking out familiar names, and sending text messages about her death. Nikiwe, whom I had met a couple of times over

172

the years when she came to visit Fikile, was one of the names. Fikile had simply introduced her as a friend from college; I did not make the link between her and Sello.

"Does she know about Bafana?"

Sello nods. "We felt our secret was safe with her."

"I don't know what to say, seeing you, hearing about Bafana, nothing makes sense right now." My heart is throbbing in my throat; I take another gulp of water.

"I'm sorry. I wish we had done things right when there was still time."

"By coming here and telling me this, now, what do you expect me to do? Fikile is not here to say what she would have wanted to see happen for the boy."

"We waited for a perfect moment to break the news, it never came. I don't want to make the same mistake again. I don't want to go to my grave not having done right with my son. Anele, I want to provide for Bafana, financially and emotionally, I want to be present for him. I want to give him the same opportunities my other children have, I want him to attend good schools with good facilities, play hockey or swim if he desires to. I want him to go to a university of his choice, here or abroad, study what he likes. I want the best for him. Most importantly, I want him to know his other blood, I want him to know he is a Mabe. I struggled so my children don't have to. I am asking you to help me achieve that. Please promise you will help me."

"Bafana has a father."

"I'm not expecting you to make sense of all of this and

make a decision now. I know it would kill me to be shut off from Bafana's life, he is the only link I have to your sister. Please, Anele, please say you'll think about what I'm asking you? I've already lost Fikile."

I wonder about the man in front of me, a man who came into my sister's life and, for a time, brought her joy. A man who is now telling me he is the father of my sister's youngest child, my nephew. My eyes unintentionally return to the couple by the poolside, the man is inside the pool now. He floats, face up, head relaxed into the water as if resting on a pillow, only his legs move lightly. I wonder how it feels to remain suspended in water as if you're a feather. I think perhaps the man is a free man, free of earthly issues and pain to weigh him down, otherwise how can he stay up like that?

The waiter comes to check on us. I look at my watch and feign an urgency to leave. I promise Sello to keep in touch.

"I will be thinking of you and your family tomorrow," Sello says.

"Thank you."

"Anele, please call me if you need something, anything, anything at all."

I leave the lodge in a dreamlike state of disorientation and with a peculiar sense of relief, like someone who has escaped a terrible motor crash unscathed. The drive home is fuzzy and long.

I ask Mvula to bring Bafana to me. He comes reeking of afternoon sun, his T-shirt is covered in orange juice, knees red with dust. I search his face for Sello Mabe: I find nothing. I do not find Thiza either. I squeeze my arms around Bafana. I tell him that I love him. Confused by the unexpected show of affection, Bafana plants a gooey kiss on my lips and wrestles out of my hold. I watch him disappear around the corner screaming Mvula's name.

Auntie Ntombi and Lesihle find me on the stoep. Auntie Ntombi scolds me for being late and not answering my phone. She asks me for the bicarbonate of soda I left to purchase. I look at her.

"Auntie forgot, again," Lesihle says with the biggest sigh of disappointment. "I told you, Gogo, that I should have gone to the shops with her."

with sympathy from all of us
at miller's trucking co.

The following day rolls out like a well-scripted play. Some mourners come in solo and in utter silence, heads bowed, fill the rows of black plastic chairs in the lounge, and speak in hushed tones to us. They sniffle in their effort to contain their emotions. They leave as quietly as they've come. Others arrive in large groups: church members from other congregations, we are one in Christ; parents of the children Fikile taught who have made an effort to organise themselves to visit Teacher Fikile's family; The Ladies of Vuka MaAfrica Society, Fikile's stokvel; parents from the children's schools; people we have never met. They enter the house with songs promising to see each other in another lifetime. They read a verse from the Bible: *Isaiah 41:10*, "So do not fear, for I am with you; do not be dismayed, for I am your God. I will strengthen you and help you; I will uphold you with my righteous right hand." They hold short sermons and leave us full of the word and hope before moving on to another aggrieved family or to commemorate with a celebrating family. Some come with a little something to leave on the collection saucer to assist us; it is no secret that funeral costs have bankrupted some families, all that waste and showing off for what?

Ma sits still in her spot at the centre of the mattress with her bad hip, flanked by Thiza's mother, and another person –

Auntie Betty, Auntie Maria, a random relative or friend. Auntie Ntombi's job is to welcome mourners, to give a reasonable account of Fikile's illness, the devious disease that continues to baffle scientists all over the world, the selfless life she lived. She does this with pride, receives each person with openness, aware these people were in some ways touched by Fikile.

Ma flaunts Mbuso at every opportunity as if to show the mourners she has not been a total failure as a mother, that something good has come out of all the disorder and destitution. She talks about his university degree, immense success in the big city, the big car and house, his return to his blood. "My boy is a man of this house now, he hasn't rested since his arrival, up and down fixing this and that, fetching this and that as his father would have done. I don't know where we would be without him around." Her eyes beam when she says this. Mbuso smiles, shakes hands with people who knew him when he was a young boy, and mumbles an excuse to leave – a fire that needs tending to, a quick trip to town, an urgent phone call he needs to return. Ma says, "You see, this is what I mean, the boy is busy, busy."

"I'll be paying for my sins for a long time, won't I?" Mbuso says to me.

I can tell he likes the attention.

Ma's friends, ex-drinking buddies, show up at random times: early in the morning as the family is waking up, water for tea not even boiled and sleep still full in our eyes, and before the elders have taken their position on the mattress;

in the middle of the day when the sun is so high up that even T-Bone cannot bother to bark at his shadow, and the house peaceful and the lure of sleep is falling on the occupants the mattress; after the last light is switched off, prayers held, and everyone has located a spot to put their heads down for a few hours. They come in a reasonable state of sobriety, sometimes with a smell of mint on their breath. They leave as unexpectedly as they come.

Thiza is a surprise. He has acquired a little stability and common sense in the few days Fikile has been dead. Like a good son-in-law he is present, only vanishing at times when he is least likely to be needed. I pretend I don't see any of his disappearing acts. He makes himself useful, even Ma is beginning to warm up to him. They caucus on the mattress, share jokes, which they laugh at quietly, privately. We have not spoken about the funeral covers and life policies he took out to cover Fikile. I know some have paid out because he placed in my hand an envelope full of cash, to help here and there, he said. We used the money to buy Fikile's tombstone. Several times I catch Thiza looking at me, not with the standard melancholy of an aggrieved but as someone filled with things unsaid. His stares unsettle me, but I pretend not to see. I pretend a lot with my brother-in-law. Alone, my conversation with Sello Mabe, neatly tucked away in a small corner of my heart, surfaces and leaves me reeling. I have not told anyone about my encounter, not even Sizwe.

Death has not made us speak softly like schemers, instead

the house hums with constant chatter and bouts of laughter that leave us reeling and gasping for air and wiping our eyes as if we're not united by grief. New stories are told, old stories retold. Family additions are introduced – a cousin, niece, a great-grandson. We join Ma and her sisters in hymns of their childhood, hymns we also grew up with. We remember dead family members, especially my father, the gentle giant taken from us before his time. The elders wonder how life would be had he lived. They fall silent, each swallowed up in their imagination of this life, until someone points out the bitter reality that we're all on our way out, and when your time is up, your time is up.

The house and its contents belong to everyone, no one can lay claim to anything, not beds or cosmetics or clothes or favourite tea cups. Mvula cries when she realises someone has squeezed a little of what is left of her bubble-gum toothpaste.

"When are we going back home? I don't want to live here anymore. Everyone must go home." Her small nostrils flare as tears stream down her face. I hide the tube of toothpaste inside the bottom drawer of Fikile's chest of drawers, promise to buy a new, big, tube after the funeral. I empathise with my daughter's fury; I too want the days to pass, so we can go back to our lives, whatever that looks like without Fikile.

Auntie Nomzamo arrives two nights before the funeral with her daughter, Zinhle, and her children. My aunt sits stiff and superior in one of the plastic chairs in the lounge. I'm glad Ma's eyes have dried; she has resorted to that faraway look she wears when life has dealt her yet another round of misery. She tilts her head slightly to the left and listens to Auntie Nomzamo lament the sudden and cruel loss of her dead brother's child, an angel.

Auntie Betty and Ntombi sit with their arms pressed against their chests, and pass each other deliberate glances. I know what they're thinking: Auntie Nomzamo didn't bother to know Fikile when she was alive, how can she care now?

Auntie Nomzamo does not speak about the funeral policy which I suspect has paid out. Zinhle had called shortly after Fikile's death to ask for a copy of her death certificate and identity number.

"I was not aware you had covered her," I said.

"Who didn't?" Zinhle said, with an easy laugh. "Don't take it the wrong way, Anele, it's not that we wanted her to die but Fikile was sick. I included her in my policy so we could contribute and support the family when the moment came. You will send me the documents when they're ready, won't you, mzala?"

I was stunned by the number of relatives who had insured my sister. I resisted at first, refused to hand out my sister's death certificate as if it were flyers one picks up at the road intersection. I lost in the end. We made a dozen copies, and yet no one has come forward with any offering. Nothing.

"They are feeding off my child's pain. Only God will judge them," Ma said.

This time I agree with Ma.

* * *

I was eleven years old when my father died after the truck he was driving collided with another truck on the highway. By the time the paramedics arrived at the scene, the bodies of both drivers had burned beyond recognition.

Ma's employers, the Hopkinses, brought her home. Ma's lifeless body was strapped in on the back seat, Mrs Hopkins, face red like a ripe tomato, holding her like a baby. Chaos followed in our household. Ma shut down for days and weeks afterwards, barely eating and talking and only wanting to sleep; Fikile tentatively took over our household. I look back at this moment as the beginning of the end of our lives.

My father's employers, Miller's Trucking Co., gave Ma a cheque of five thousand rands for her loss. Five thousand rands was a figure that featured in family discussions for months, years. None of the white people came to the funeral, not even Meneer Retief, whom my father fondly had referred to as *Groot Oom Baas*, who had given him fruit and vegetables past their prime from his smallholding every Christmas. Instead the company sent a big bouquet of flowers, and a card, white with silver wording: *With Sympathy From All of Us at Miller's Trucking Co.* This I knew because all I was able to do during my father's funeral was look at the flowers sitting on top of the wooden coffin, the biggest bunch of flowers I had ever seen. They were beautiful, like they belonged at a wedding; I thought it was wasteful to have them at the funeral and had tasked myself to make sure the flowers got back to our house after we buried my father. The card fell off as my uncles lifted the coffin. I picked it up and clutched it in my small hands. My stomach was a ball of nerves, I kept thinking someone was going to scold me and demand I give it back. No one did, not even when the men had lowered the coffin into the ground and we were asked to scoop a handful of soil from the shovel and pour it over the coffin.

I did not attempt to collect the flowers lying in a mound of red soil and rock, my father's grave, when we left.

No one asked for the card when we got home, eating food that was so delicious it could be mistaken for Sunday lunch, prepared by my mother's stokvel. I hid the soggy card in my schoolbag and took it out every day, smoothing it with my hands, until it started to peel and the white glossy paper became grey and coarse. The words were faint, illegible, but I had memorised them, *With Sympathy from All of Us at Miller's Trucking Co.*

One day I found Mbuso playing with my schoolbag; the card was gone. I slapped him hard on each cheek, screaming for *my* card. Mbuso had not cried straightaway, instead he looked at me, eyes bulging, unable to move. I pointed a finger at him and told him never to play with my schoolbag again. I started packing my stuff back inside the bag – an unsharpened pencil, a blue pen, a broken ruler, three brown covered exercise books – when unexpectedly Mbuso let out a piercing scream that brought Ma running to the room. She took one look at the wailing child and lunged at me.

It was two months since my father's passing, two months

I had not seen Ma's eyes empty of tears, two months I had not seen Ma sober. I jumped over my bed and was out of the door before Ma's hand could close on me. I ran as fast as I could and only stopped when my legs buckled. I sat on the side of the road, watching cars and trucks whiz by, wishing they could take me with them. Ma was acting strange, and had stopped being Ma, and had turned into someone I didn't recognise. She had also developed a temper we hadn't known before. We were all scared of her.

When it was getting dark, I turned around and slowly started to make my way back, resigned to Ma's wrath and the punishment to be unleashed on me. When I reached home, Mbuso was waiting for me at the gate; he seemed pleased to see me. He offered his hand and I took it.

"Is Ma still angry?"

Mbuso shook his head no. I didn't believe him.

"I'm sorry I hit you, but you must stop touching my things without asking me. Promise?"

"I promise," Mbuso said, and produced a slightly crumpled and wet card.

I snatched it from his hand, and turned it over, inspecting the damages. When I was satisfied with its condition, I put it in my pocket. "Where was it?"

"In the bag. The card was in the bag the whole time."

"I'm sorry, okay."

Hand in hand we walked towards the house, my heart pounding. Fikile was in the kitchen and had started boiling water for pap. She glanced at me and said it's dangerous for a girl my age to be on the streets on her own so late. I apologised, told her I was scared of Ma. She said I shouldn't worry about Ma, that I should go check what I could find in the garden. I led Mbuso outside to the back towards the small vegetable patch I had started as a school gardening project and selected a few leaves of spinach.

* * *

Auntie Ntombi keeps Fikile's bedroom locked. It is doubling up as a storage room where food and items of value are kept – plasma television, dvd player, Thiza's stereo – even our handbags are banished here.

It is in this room where I find my two aunts surrounded by cans of baked beans, bags of rice, sauces and spices, and a dozen two-litre bottles of cold drink. I have come to scoop maize meal to prepare the evening pap. I tap lightly at the door and open without waiting for a response. I catch Auntie Betty mid-sentence:

"– I can't say I'm surprised, he is a vindictive man. But sisi we warned you. We were so shocked that out of all the potential handsome suitors, and there were many, you chose that old, shrewd man," Auntie Betty chuckles.

"I'm sorry," I say backing out of the room, but Auntie Ntombi waves me in.

"Come in, baby. Close the door."

My aunts are lying on the bed, heads resting on the wooden headboard, arms folded over their tummies, Auntie Ntombi's wide hips sprawled like a mountain.

"I won't be long," I say as I negotiate my way to the corner of the room where bags of maize meal have been emptied into a large sealable plastic drum.

"What can I say, I was young and blinded by love. I didn't know the story would end with us dragging each other to courts and wasting money."

I'm reminded that when Auntie Ntombi announced her divorce to the family a year ago, after being Uncle Joseph's wife for twenty-five years, we all thought she had uttered the word "divorce" by mistake. I did not know anyone of her age who got divorced. Aunties carried the strains of their marriages in their tight doeks covering their heads, with each sip of sweet milky tea drunk in private in the wee hours of the morning, in their neatly pressed church uniforms as they hugged other congregants, uttering, "Go in peace." But they never left their matrimonial homes. And besides, Uncle Joseph was as part of our lives as the green Gommagommas in our living room.

"Divorce?" Ma had exclaimed.

"We will not be the first people to break up, sisi," Auntie Ntombi said in the tight voice I had heard her use on some of the children at her school.

"We were not aware that you were having problems," Ma said. "You never said anything to anyone."

"I have been unhappy for some time now. In all honesty, I'm at the end of my wits trying to rationalise and having conversations with myself on why I should stay. I'm tired of doing all the emotional work to keep our relationship going."

Auntie Betty snorted, "Good riddance."

I remember Auntie Ntombi's long conversations with Ma weeks after that, hushed words full of questions and affirmations, my aunt's soft cries. The distance between the sisters had narrowed following Fikile's illness and Ma quitting alcohol, such that Auntie Ntombi's presence in our house did not trigger an avalanche of mutters and dread.

I was once fond of Uncle Joseph, our well-dressed, English-speaking uncle who holds a very important job at the local Home Affairs office. We spent a couple of school holidays at Auntie Ntombi's house, until the year Fikile and I stopped going and only Mbuso continued to visit. We loved visiting Auntie Ntombi's house. Her house was more complete than ours, even the garage was tiled and had cupboards where Auntie Ntombi kept tools to prune her roses. At Auntie Ntombi's we ate eggs for breakfast and meat for dinner. Every day.

Uncle Joseph delighted in taking us with our cousin in his green Toyota Corolla for a drive to town where we would stop at the café and buy fish and chips and fresh white bread and Fanta orange. Or to the game reserve where he taught us how to spot giraffes and elephants. Once, Uncle Joseph insisted on taking only Fikile and Mbuso to the shops, and I was banished to helping my aunt in the garden. They were gone for no more than an hour. My heart overflowed with jealousy so much that I did not speak to Fikile when they returned. Fikile retaliated to my silent treatment by saying it was fine if I didn't speak to her because she did not want to talk to me or anyone in the house. She only wore her pair of long jeans and covered her body in long-sleeved shirts after that, and would not change into a dress or skirt even when Auntie Ntombi threatened to take her home. "Teenagers, they think they know everything," my aunt would say in surrender. Fikile was fifteen, the first summer of our father's death.

When the next school holidays came, Fikile announced casually that she was staying behind. I was shocked. I demanded a reason. Fikile said she wanted to stay home and look after Ma. My sister's justification was suspicious. Even I knew that she and Ma did not get along. I couldn't understand why she would choose to stay with her. For days leading up to the school closure, I pleaded with my sister to reconsider, promised to submit to her all through the holidays, and when she said she wasn't changing her mind, in my frustration I screamed at her and told her she was selfish and ruining my holiday.

"Anele, go if you want. I'm not stopping you," Fikile said in that sharp tone she sometimes used with Ma, a tone that made Ma stop talking, look up at her adolescent daughter with a mixture of indignation and defeat, and leave the room without saying another word.

When Uncle Joseph came to pick us up, three days after the schools closed, only Mbuso brought out his small bag. I remember the look of surprise on Uncle Joseph's face at the sight of Fikile and I in our house dresses, hair uncombed and with no indication of departure. He turned to Ma.

"Are the girls not joining us?" he asked with that patient voice of his.

Ma shrugged, said, "They want to stay home this time, Joseph."

We watched our uncle reverse the car out of our yard, Mbuso waving happily from the back seat.

"We will have fun, I promise," Fikile said to me, her voice full of satisfaction. She wrapped her arms around my heaving body. I was so overwhelmed with regret I almost ran after the car.

It turned out to be a magical summer. When I wasn't riding my bike, a gift from Uncle Majaha for my birthday, or playing *maroundas* and *touch* with my friends, I joined my sister and her friends under the giant fever tree by the gate. They let me listen to their conversations and allowed me to go with them to the shopping centre where they bought caramel-dipped ice cream cones and cold drinks and pretended not to want to speak to boys. I forgot about my anger towards my sister. I was so content that I never did ask Fikile why she did not want to go to Auntie Ntombi's house. We hardly visited our aunt's house after that.

My ears prick up as Auntie Ntombi explains that their estate is under contestation and she isn't bending. "I want what I deserve."

"Which is everything," Auntie Betty says.

"He will not win, I'll die first."

I remain glued on the spot between the maize meal drum and the door. I can feel Auntie Betty's eyes on me. I know what she's thinking, later she will give me another lecture on how men are here on earth to spread their seeds and wreak havoc. I hurriedly scoop enough to fill the large bowl I'm carrying and leave the room.

* * *

Mbuso and I are driving to town to buy a decent black dress for Ma and a suit for Bafana.

"I didn't realise the amount of work it takes to prepare a funeral," Mbuso comments. "I'm used to showing up on the day in my black suit and charm."

"It's work. I miss sleep. I miss sleeping in my bed more than anything."

"It's almost over."

"The distraction has been more than welcome, though. I'm nervous about Saturday, once everyone has packed up and left, what will we do?"

"I'll be here."

"Ma will like that."

There is a silence, which neither of us tries to fill. Then Mbuso says, quite mildly, "It didn't work out between me and Mapule. Our divorce was finalised eight months ago."

"I'm sorry. What happened?"

"My marriage was a perfect disaster, actually." Mbuso throws his head back against the headrest as he says this. "I suppose the appropriate question is what didn't happen? The short answer is I couldn't give Mapule what she wanted, deserved, I couldn't share a part of me with her. I was selfishly licking scabs and opening old wounds that should have been left to heal on their own. I forgot to live in the present."

I make an encouraging sound to acknowledge that I'm hearing him. I recall the phone call from Mbuso's now ex-wife those many years ago, shortly after their wedding, desperation in her voice. She apologised, said it was not her intention to drag her husband's family into her marital life. She had no one else to turn to. She wanted to know the root of Mbuso's anger. She said Mbuso was impossible to understand.

"He won't let me in. We fight over small, silly things, but instead of resolving issues like normal married people, Mbuso dismisses me, shuts me out. Sometimes he barely says a word for days, weeks. On those days, it is like living with a tree, can you imagine sharing a house with someone who doesn't see you? You know what's funny? I'm a medical doctor, I'm supposed to know how to heal people, but I'm failing in my own home. I can't heal my husband. I can't heal my marriage and I don't know what to do." Between sniffles, she said she wanted to know what happened, why he never came home to visit, why he shunned his family. "Whatever trauma it was I can handle. Was he abused as a child or something?"

I explained to Mbuso's wife about our father's untimely death and Ma's subsequent problem with alcohol. "Mbuso felt neglected and has been angry with our mother ever since, in fact, he is mad at everyone. He was only a little boy when it happened, and Fikile and I were also just children. We couldn't replace our parents' love and care. Our mother is sober now." I was careful not to add that it was possible Mbuso was simply being selfish, holding onto ancient grudges like he was the only one with a wounded childhood, like Fikile had not sold herself to provide for us. "I can talk to Mbuso if you want."

Mapule declined the offer, said she didn't want Mbuso to even know she had called. "I'm scared of how he will react, it might make things worse. Let's rather keep this conversation to ourselves, okay? I don't want to lose your brother, Anele. I love him too much. If only he would talk to me, I could help him."

I had debated calling my brother to talk to him anyway. Although I thought I knew the bottom of Mbuso's problems, ours wasn't the type of relationship where I could pick up a phone and say, "Okay little bro, come on, cut the crap and let's fix your marriage." I did not want to risk further alienating Mbuso. In the end, I did not make the phone call.

Mbuso looks at me sidelong in the car. "I can't fault Mapule in any of this, she tried with me, and to some degree made me happy. My reasons for marrying were wrong to begin with, I sought out marriage to bring me a feeling of completeness. I saw it as the only thing that could fill the missing gaps in my life and wipe away my solitude forever. I was educated and financially secured, all I needed was a wife, a few kids, a nice house, a perfect setting, and I could create the family environment I never had. My perfect family. But clearly that was not enough."

"Do you have children?" It is a strange thing to ask my brother this.

Mbuso shakes his head. "Mapule fell pregnant, and we felt hope return. I don't think I've ever seen her happier than when a life was growing in her belly. A few weeks before she was due to deliver our child, a baby girl, whom we had named Kagiso, I woke up to her growling with pain from abdominal cramps. I rushed her to the hospital but she lost the baby. She was never right after that. One day she packed her bags and moved back with her parents. She said it was temporary, while she dealt with the loss and cleared her head. Deep down in our hearts we knew our marriage was over."

"I'm sorry, that must have been rough."

"I won't lie, those days were full of haze and confusion. I know my friends, our friends, regarded me with a tinge of blame. Then something incredible happened, I woke up one morning to a great sense of liberty and pleasure, the kind I last experienced when I stepped inside the university gates. You see, I didn't have the guts to walk out on Mapule, I could never be the one to cause that pain."

I must look mortified because Mbuso's voice is full of anxiety and appeasement, "You must think I'm a horrible person? I abandoned you and I've done the same with Mapule."

"Do you know that Mapule came to see us?"

My brother shakes his head, steals another glance in my direction.

"I'm guessing this was before she fell pregnant. Or maybe she was already expecting, I don't know, she didn't say, and I didn't see anything. She said she wanted to meet the family, wanted to know whom she'd married, our people, where you come from. She said maybe if she knew us, connected with us, she would understand you better."

* * *

Mbuso went and arranged his lobolo. He sent friends and elderly colleagues, random people not known to us, as his representatives. This we heard about from a neighbour's friend who was not part of the delegation himself but friends with one of abakhongi. He had wondered, the friend said, looking rather troubled, why Uncle Majaha and Auntie Betty were not involved. The things young people do, he added. Nine months later, Mbuso called, inviting Fikile and I to his wedding.

"What about Ma? What about the rest of the family?" I demanded. I could somehow excuse him organising his own lobolo, but denying Ma the wedding was cruel.

"Not a good idea to bring her. I don't want to humiliate myself in front of people," Mbuso answered sharply.

"What are you saying, Mbuso? Are you ashamed of us?"

"Please, Anele, let's not get into an argument over this, you know what I mean. Nothing is predictable with Ma. Please, say you will come."

"And others?"

"Look, it's a small ceremony for close friends and family

members. We're thinking of doing something later for everyone who can't join us for this leg of the wedding."

Even as he was saying those words, I knew Mbuso was only trying to appease me; there would be no such arrangement.

"Please, say you will come," he said again.

"I'll speak to Fikile."

Fikile said absolutely not. She said Mbuso was insulting the family.

I begged her to reconsider until she reluctantly agreed.

"I'm only agreeing so I can tell Mbuso in person how I feel about the whole thing," Fikile said.

We announced the wedding to the family. Auntie Betty clapped her hands and said she was washing her hands of Mbuso. Ma came back from a drinking spree spewing expletives directed at my absent brother. Auntie Ntombi shook her head and said, "Mbuso must really hate us. How could he do such a thing to us?"

We drove out on the morning of the wedding; the ceremony was planned for the afternoon at an exclusive venue. A modern wedding, the wedding invite – which Mbuso later sent to me via email – stated: *Mr and Mrs Molefe have the pleasure of inviting you to the wedding of their daughter Dr Mapule Molefe to Mbuso Mabuza, son of the late Mr and Mrs M. Mabuza, at The Palms Conference Centre. We regret no children allowed.*

Mbuso met us at the entrance of the venue.

We had last seen him at his graduation which Fikile and

I attended with Auntie Ntombi and Uncle Joseph. After the graduation ceremony, Mbuso had treated us to lunch at a nearby hotel. Over a curry buffet, with naan, and poppadoms, he announced that he had accepted a job with an Australian firm and that he would be flying out the following day to begin orientation. Auntie Ntombi stopped chewing and dropped her fork on the side of her plate. She had been planning Mbuso's big surprise party since receiving a call from him that he graduated top in his class.

"We were hoping to celebrate the moment with everyone back home. Everyone is so proud of you, Mbuso. Can't you postpone your trip for another week?"

It was too late, he couldn't postpone, the flights had been booked, accommodation arranged. He was so sorry.

"Maybe when I return in six months?"

Auntie Ntombi looked as if she was about to burst into tears.

"I will return, Auntie, the contract is only for six months." Mbuso went over to hug her, promised again to return.

At his wedding, Mbuso stood in front of us, arms wide open, his face plastered in a ready smile.

"You can hang out here, order anything you want, anything, make yourself comfortable. I'll meet you later." He said he had a few errands to complete before the big *event*.

The bride was beautiful, the groom immaculate. The ceremony was sophisticated and dazzling. The young couple smiled and laughed as they made their rounds to the guests' tables, chanting, "We are so happy you came."

And finally, they made it to our table.

"And these are very special people, my sisters, Fikile and Anele," Mbuso said. "My wife, Mapule."

A look of surprise from the bride. "Oh, hello, so pleased to meet you. I didn't know you were here. Baby, you forgot to tell me your sisters were coming. I could have met them earlier and –"

"They've just got in, babe. Don't worry, you will have plenty of time to get to know them." A smile from the groom. A gentle push to the right. Time to move to another table.

Hours later when the formalities were concluded, wedding guests enjoying the free bar, and dancing to house music and kwaito and R&B on the black-and-white chequered floor, the bride and her mother made their way to our table.

"We are happy you made it," the mother of the bride said, beaming with pride. "We have begged Mbuso for months to meet his family. I have been saying, nobody is born out of a tree, we all belong somewhere. Family is the centre of our existence."

"We are there," Fikile said with a slight irritation in her voice. "Mbuso's family is all there."

"I never doubted that," Mapule's mother laughed. "Mom couldn't make it? Mbuso told us she was unwell."

Fikile and I stole a careful look at each other. "Yes, she is still unwell," I managed a response.

"That's a pity, we would have liked to meet her but we're glad you are here. Tomorrow we must sit and choose a day to properly bring our daughter over to the Mabuza home. The Molefes are traditional and still observe our cultural practices. Between us, I must admit the kids took us by surprise with this wedding, look at them, both so young. But what can we say, they're inseparable."

Mapule pulled me aside. "Anele, I'm so happy to finally meet you. My husband speaks a lot about you. Please take my number and buzz me so I have yours," she said, smiling.

In the taxi on our way home I told Fikile I sensed sadness and desperation in her voice. Fikile said she wasn't surprised, she said she doubted if Mbuso was capable of loving and truly giving with all that anger.

More relatives flocked to our table.

"Oh, Mbuso's sisters? I didn't know he had sisters. How are you?"

And then, the groom. Mbuso's joy floated and bounced around the room like an inflated balloon. I had forgotten his laughter; my brother spent his years with us swallowed in sourness.

Mbuso arranged for us to sleep at his house, a massive structure inside a golf country estate. There were other people in the house who arrived after us, friends of the groom, strangers to us. We left early the following morning.

Fikile was furious. She refused to speak to Mbuso until several years later when she fell sick and I called him in a panic.

* * *

In the car, I tell Mbuso how everyone was excited at the prospect of finally meeting Mapule after she confirmed her visit; how our aunts laboured in the kitchen preparing a lunch fit for the *queen* as they joked, while Ma paced the yard picking up dead leaves. She had not slept the night before, and had checked the large clock in the kitchen every few minutes.

"Where is she now?" she asked me.

"Close, Ma."

When Mapule's car pulled in, we ululated and sang and hugged her and planted kisses on her red-coloured lips. We marked her as ours.

Mapule brought a gift for everyone – luxurious wool throws, seshweshe outfits, and sparkling cutlery for the women; toys and books for the children; and long, black trench coats for Uncle Majaha and Thiza. We ululated even louder, our makoti came prepared.

"Mbuso thinks I'm at my parents this weekend. I visit them often," Mapule said when we were alone in my room. She held my hand as she spoke. "I'm glad I'm here, Anele. All I know about your family is from snippets of conversations with your brother, I've picked up an aunt and uncle here, nieces and nephews there, a memory somewhere. I have been going insane trying to piece together his history, your history. It never used to bother me much that Mbuso had not brought me to meet his family when we were dating. I'm older now, I need to know. And when we start having children, I can't bring them into this life while in the dark.

What would I tell my child if she asked about her aunts and paternal grandparents, her clan names? You see, I needed to come."

Later I showed Mapule old family albums. She asked questions as she turned the pages, and laughed at Mbuso's younger pictures. When she was finished, she asked if she could keep one photo of my brother, aged eleven or twelve, before the dark years.

"Thank you," she said, holding back tears. Mapule knew then we loved Mbuso.

"Did he tell you how we met?"

"No."

"I thought *I* was driven until I met your brother. We met at university, at a library. I guess we were those nerdy people who waited impatiently for the library doors to open and got annoyed when they announced closing time. Mbuso wasn't shy, but preferred to keep to himself. I had to drag him out to the movies or dinner. But he was always sure of the life he wanted for himself, and he never lost focus."

Mapule spent two days with us and left with a promise to return, with Mbuso this time. It was the last time I spoke to my sister-in-law. Between Fikile's chemotherapy and getting on with the business of everyday life, I forgot about her.

And now a tiny part of me blames my cowardice for my brother's failed marriage.

I glance at his ringless hand on the steering wheel. "Mbuso, you have unanswered questions which you've tried to sweep under the carpet, hoping they will disappear. Maybe you need to have a frank conversation with Ma, maybe that will help."

Mbuso nods, says, "Ma."

"Don't forget we also got the raw end of the deal, all of us, including Ma. You can't be hard on her. She is an old woman who has had a shitty life, self-inflicted or not. Imagine waking up every day feeling inadequate and worthless. She can't sleep, has these dreams that have been tormenting her for years involving Baba. In her dreams, he is unkind and snubs her. You see, Ma believes that she and Dad would meet and resume their lives again. It's awful."

"I didn't know." He is silent for a while. "Okay, enough about me and my failures. Sizwe seems like a decent guy, what is the plan? Is there marriage on the cards? More kids?"

"I don't know. I'm stuck, it feels like my life is stagnant, that every few steps forward, I take ten steps back. Sometimes I wonder if my sole purpose in this life is to take care of other people's happiness. Like that's my job, except maybe I don't want that job. I know it sounds terrible and –"

"No, you're right, you've sacrificed a lot for all of us."

"And that's the thing, there is no end in sight. What's going to happen in a couple of days once everyone has gone back to their lives?"

"I want you to know that I will never leave you alone again. I will do my best to help raise Fikile's children and take care of Ma, okay? You are not alone anymore."

"Thank you."

"We will be fine."

thank you, baba

We are two days away from burying Fikile. It is late afternoon, I itch to escape the pandemonium at my sister's place. There are humans everywhere, and the air is rich in sweet smells of freshly baked queen cakes and fermenting sorghum and sweat. No one cries now; it is as if our tears caucused and decided to take a long-deserved break. We welcome the reprieve. On occasions when grief falls upon us, we swallow it with a sigh and short silence, sometimes someone breaks into song, a common hymn, one verse and the order is restored. We don't feel the warm nights roll by.

I collect the overflowing laundry baskets and make my way to my mother's house. I take my time to sort and wash and put the clothes on the washing line to dry. Laundry days were special at our house. Fikile and I woke up every Saturday, filled large steel washing basins with soap and water. Fikile washed, while I rinsed and added fabric softener when we had some. I helped Fikile peg sheets and our uniforms, a row of white and khaki shirts, khaki shorts, and black skirts. Twice a year we washed the blankets, Mbuso and I stamped on them until they were clean. While the laundry dried, we rewarded ourselves with a hearty breakfast of buttered bread, thick polony slices and atchar, washed down with juice. As I got older, I took over the laundry with Mbuso as my reluctant assistant.

I'm at the back, picking clothes from the washing line when I hear Sizwe's car splutter and pull up in the front yard. I can hear his car from miles away. He saved money for two years to buy a used double-cab bakkie, which he has proceeded to spend a chunk of his wages fixing. Without fail, no sooner has he replaced a part – a blown gasket, gearbox, short-circuiting reverse light – than another part collapses. Umgodoyi, Sizwe calls his car on bad days, Dali on good days; it's a love-hate relationship I've chosen not to be part of.

When the car engine dies, I hear the doors open and shut. A few minutes later, Sizwe, followed by a woman with a child in tow, emerges from the other side of the house. I register the look of surprise on his face when he sees me. I stop and watch as the three figures deposit themselves in front of me. Sizwe is holding a worn-out denim schoolbag bursting at the seams. It isn't his. When the woman is closer, I look at her hard, trying to place her, thinking perhaps it's someone I have seen at his friends' parties, at the local shops, at the municipality offices. Or maybe someone I met through Fikile, and who has come to pay her respects to the deceased. The woman is wearing a long, black cotton maxi dress with short sleeves and slightly worn-out sandals. Her head is covered in a neat colourful head wrap. I don't know her, I conclude. My eyes move down to the child, a boy, two or three years older than Mvula. The boy won't stop tugging at the woman's hem. I smile at him, he peers out and immediately dives back behind the woman's dress.

Sizwe introduces the woman and the child, names which elude me when I search for them later. I nod my head to the woman but her eyes are fixed on Sizwe, in a glare. Both her hands are clutching a black carry-on bag. The woman whispers something to Sizwe.

"They are hungry," he says, his eyes avoiding mine.

I know Sizwe has a younger sister who was raised by his aunts when their parents passed on when they were children, he said he wasn't close to his sister the way he was with his older brother, Paul. But there is no resemblance to this woman, no trace of Mthembu blood – she is darker, her skin the colour of stained wood. She is easily one of the most beautiful women I have laid my eyes on. I quickly remind myself of the unpredictability of genes, me and Mbuso, for example, nothing screams sibling relations about us no matter how much one searches for clues.

"Your sister?"

"No." I think I hear her say.

"I will explain later. Do we have food?"

I finish taking down the clothes from the line, fold and place them in the two washing baskets and go inside the house to search for something to eat for our guests. Sizwe follows carrying the baskets, as do the woman and the boy. We have no bread or milk or eggs or vegetables; we emptied the fridge and took everything to Fikile's house. Even the relatives who come here to sleep in the evenings congregate at Fikile's for breakfast and homemade dinners. Sizwe finds concentrated mango juice in the cardboard and mixes it with water. I watch the woman and the boy gulp it down. I turn to Sizwe, but he has his back to me and is looking out towards the back rooms. I boil water and stir in maize meal. The woman stands, offers to help, but I wave her to sit back down. The boy's body is facing the living room, watching the television at an angle. He is asking Sizwe questions – Can he go watch? Can he –? Why is –? Sizwe's responses are brisk, sometimes the child says the same thing over and over until the woman hisses at him. He becomes quiet for a second only to start again. I steal glances at the woman whose eyes are glued on Sizwe with such intensity she makes him fidget and change his position several times. She looks down when she catches me looking at her.

I prepare a gravy of canned fish in tomato sauce and baked beans, the only items I can find. I take out two plates and dish up for the guests. Sizwe leans on the doorframe, smoking a cigarette in nervous puffs and blowing the smoke outside. I place the food in front of them, apologising for the basic meal, and leave the kitchen.

Waves of exhaustion cascade through my body as I collapse on the couch. I yearn for Sizwe's firm fingers pressing on my feet. I hear Sizwe say something, the woman says something back, and the little boy replies, "Thank you, Baba."

Baba?

A children's cartoon programme is on, I half-watch, half-strain to eavesdrop on the conversation in the kitchen, though I can't pick up much, they are both managing to keep their voices down. I scroll through my phone and land on Eunice's number, dial and drop. What would I say to her? We have guests, a woman and her child, the boy just called Sizwe Baba?

The scraping of the plates is a good indication of the guests' appetites. I hear the sound of liquid being poured. After a few minutes the boy slips shyly into the lounge, eyes glued to the television. The woman calls out after him but he does not respond. I watch him sit on the floor next to my feet. He looks up at me with big yellowish eyes and smiles, then turns back to the television. I hear the woman push her chair back, followed by running water. She and Sizwe are talking rapidly, her voice slightly raised, Sizwe's charged with repressed anger. I hear Sizwe's footsteps approach the lounge. He tells the boy to follow him.

The boy does not stir.

"Leave him for a bit, he is enjoying himself," I plead on his behalf.

"Mxolisi!"

Mxolisi flinches, reluctantly stands and follows Sizwe out of the room, eyes still straining to catch what he can.

After a few minutes Sizwe returns, sits next to me.

"You should have let him watch," I say.

"They are tired."

"Who are they?"

Sizwe takes a deep breath, shakes his head, slowly.

"Sizwe, who are they?"

"My wife, my ex-wife – soon to be ex-wife – and my boy. I wasn't completely honest with you about my past and I'm ashamed. I never divorced my wife. Legally, I'm still married, though that marriage means nothing to me. Nothing. You must believe me," he says sharply.

"What are you saying, Sizwe?" A small laugh squeezes out of my mouth involuntarily and floats around the room until it dissipates. "What are you saying? You don't have a wife. You don't have a son."

"I just left," he says. "I left her. I woke up one day and packed my things and left. I didn't know about the child, I swear."

* * *

Sizwe first came to our house years back selling his handyman services – plumbing, construction, electrical, anything that needed fixing or building he could do, he said. He handed me a small black and white flyer listing the services and his contact details. I had listened politely, and when I thought he was finished told him I didn't have work for him. Sizwe noticed the half-built room structure at the back of the house, and stacks of cement bricks next to it, some crumbling at the edges for lack of use. He pointed at the room with interest. He could finish building for me, cheap, professional work I would not be disappointed in, he said.

I shook my head. "I don't have money to buy material, let alone pay the builder."

"But I will do it cheaply for you," he said, his voice desperate.

"I'm sorry, I don't have money to build right now. Nothing."

He wanted to know more about the rooms, were we extending the house or looking to rent them out? I had started building the back rooms to rent them out, the space at the back of our house was big enough to fit another house. Besides, I needed the extra money. Ma was not old enough to qualify for government pension and her refusal to sober up and return to work placed the job of maintaining our household, even after Mbuso had left, squarely on my shoulders. The rental income, I reasoned, would be sufficient to sustain Ma after I left to start my life elsewhere.

"There is no money," I repeated to Sizwe.

"I understand, you have no money now. I will come back at the end of the month, we can talk then."

I shrugged. "No, I still won't have money. Come back end of the year, maybe I will have saved enough by then."

Sizwe appeared to consider this, but then suddenly said he wanted to make a deal, he would complete the room in exchange for boarding for two months or three months afterwards. And then he would go, not disturb me again.

"You're not listening, I do not have money to buy the material needed to complete the building." I said this out slowly to aid his comprehension.

Sizwe shook his head, waved me off. "No, no, no worries, you have enough material here, I will organise the rest. We will build fast, three weeks and the room will be finished. Deal?"

To get rid of him, I asked Sizwe to come back at the end of the month.

"Ok, ok," he said, smiling. "Can I drink some water?" He pointed at the tap by the boulders.

"Sure." I watched him bend and take long gulps, and splash water on his face and hair. He had on faded blue jeans with holes on the knees and worn construction boots. The heat had left his jet-black hair stuck to his scalp like a newborn's hair, sweat dripped down his face, soaking the blue-and-white Hawaiian shirt. His body was lean and masculine, I guessed his age to be about thirty-two, thirty-five maximum.

"Month end," he said and waved goodbye and walked away.

Sizwe returned two weeks later. I was not home. He waited outside the gate the entire afternoon, and when he saw me approach, opened the gate, and walked with me towards the house.

"Remember me? Sizwe. I will build for you." His face was hopeful and pleading. He was in the same outfit I'd previously seen him in. "I have the material. Tomorrow I will come and we will build, fast."

I surprised myself by agreeing to Sizwe's proposal. Later I told Ma.

"Maybe he knows someone who works at a hardware store," she said.

They were at the house at the crack of dawn the following day, Sizwe and two other men he introduced as cousins. They came in a white battered bakkie crammed with bags of cement and sand.

"See, see, I told you I will make a plan. Now we build," Sizwe said, gleeful.

I did not ask where the material came from or if they were really related or if they even knew how to lay bricks.

"I don't want trouble," I warned Sizwe before I left for work. "Here is my cell number if you need to get hold of me."

"No trouble, I promise. We're good people."

"Here, I made juice and bread for you. I'll leave it by the veranda."

He hesitated. "We don't want to trouble you."

"It's only bread and juice. Please, take it, just for today." The food was Ma's idea.

I told my friend Eunice about the men building a room at the back of our house in exchange for boarding.

"Smells like a scam, what if they build and move in and never want to leave? What if he is using stolen material? Tell them to stop straightaway, tell them the deal is cancelled or this won't end well for someone. Anyway, where has he been all this time, where does he come from? I've never seen him around."

"He's been living with his older brother."

"Still stinks of trouble to me. I'm surprised you've agreed to this."

"I'll be careful, promise."

Sizwe and his men worked fast and meticulously. On weekends, I watched them from the kitchen window. They spoke all the time and laughed and sang maskandi songs. They spoke as if they had known each other for a long time,

I began to think perhaps they really were related or came from the same town.

I cooked extra food in the evenings – porridge, chicken, spinach, minced meat, beans – whatever we had, and left it out for them. Each time they protested, but Ma insisted they eat our food.

Sizwe wanted to add a small room adjacent to the bedroom they were building. "Where will the people bath?" he asked when I resisted. "You can't expect your tenants to wash in small basins in their rooms as if they're in the hostels. You must make this place nice so you can earn good money."

Each day Ma and I watched the walls go up, then the roof with its tiny sheet. True to his word, Sizwe finished building in three weeks – the dull concrete structure, with a second-hand door freshly painted red. We inspected the rooms, Ma and I, and were pleased.

"They have a neat hand," Ma exclaimed, touching the smooth plaster.

Sizwe moved in shortly thereafter, bringing with him a thin mattress, some blankets, a two-plate stove, two wobbly-looking plastic chairs, a small wooden table, a green bucket and matching washing basin, and a portable radio. He seemed pleased with his space. On his first night, he sat outside until late playing music and smoking a joint. I would later learn more and fall in love with maskandi.

Sizwe's presence in our lives was an unexpected welcome. My father had died before I could appreciate his contribution, and Mbuso had left too young, before he was useful to us. Sizwe collected ripe fruit from the many trees in the yard and placed them in baskets and delivered them to me or Ma. He raked leaves, fixed the leaking roof in the garage, and repaired the broken furniture around the house. With the left-over cement from the building, he filled the holes in the floor all over the house, plastered its walls, and promised to find cheap paint. We had not done major work around the house since we moved in those many years go.

Ma started calling him "son" and in her drunken state told him how she wished he was her son, and how her real son had deserted her and thought he was better than everybody because he had a university education and a fancy office job. Sizwe held her when she cried for Mbuso.

As the year progressed, Sizwe began to build the other two rooms. I could save a little each month for material then, a few bags of cement here, a doorframe there, until, after a year, the construction was complete. A young police constable rented one of the rooms, and we kept the other one for Mbuso even though we were not certain if he would return home.

One evening I found Sizwe waiting for me in his friend's old car outside my work. He said he happened to pass by. He opened the door for me. He smelled nice, lemongrass and musk. He was unusually quiet during the ride home, and when we arrived, as I was preparing to get out, he gave me a look I had never seen on him, firm and assured, and said, "You should be my woman." I was so startled for a moment that I couldn't find words to respond. I stared him down. He averted his eyes, withdrawing like a hurt puppy. I got out of the car without saying another word. I couldn't sleep that night. Sizwe?

Sizwe was outside the door of our house the next morning. He offered me a lift, asked if I had given his proposal some thought. I laughed, and said he hadn't proposed, "You commanded me to be your woman." I told him we wouldn't work, that we were different. He said from what he could see, we were not that different.

"In any case, I'm not looking for a relationship."

Sizwe seemed to ponder this. "Ok, *you* may not be looking, but that doesn't mean I'm not looking either."

Later that evening he grilled chicken for us. Ma loved Sizwe's piri-piri chicken, which he had taken to preparing for us on weekends. Growing up in northern KwaZulu-Natal he said he had spent time in Mozambique and learned the skills to master the *frango*. Sometimes he grilled fresh tilapia, which he bought from the fish shop in town. We were in the kitchen, I was cutting the warm chicken into pieces while he leaned by the doorframe smoking. We shared snippets of our histories and harboured dreams. He had left everything back home to start a new life, the reason he was desperate for a room. He asked about Mbuso a lot.

"You really need to stop smoking," I said.

"I'll stop if you give me your heart."

"Well, then, go ahead and kill yourself."

He stubbed out the cigarette and washed his hands in the

tap outside. I handed him his half of the chicken in a plate. He came close, so close I could smell the smoke from his skin. He touched the side of my cheek with the back of his hand, ran his fingers down my neck to my breast, and gave it a light squeeze. I froze. I knew then the pretence that he was just Sizwe, the tenant with handyman skills, was quickly dissolving. I threw my head back and groaned. I had missed a man's touch. We ate our chicken in the garage and made love into the early hours of the morning.

Months later Ma sat us down and said there was no need for Sizwe to continue living like a boarder, she said he was more family than our own blood relatives. He moved inside the main house shortly after that. Ma had found her replacement son. Mvula came along eighteen months later.

* * *

Sizwe and I don't speak for a while. I close and open my eyes hoping I'm in a bad dream, that the father of my child did not just tell me he has a whole family, a whole world that doesn't involve us. I close and open my eyes, and see Sizwe next to me, squeezing my leg, my arm, my hand, and whispering, "I'm sorry. I was a coward to walk away from my responsibilities and for not being straight with you from the beginning. I don't know, I thought you wouldn't want me if you knew the truth."

I never asked him for more than he shared, I never had reason to. I took his words to be true and complete. He had left a failed relationship. He did not keep in touch with the woman, her choice. He left his hometown to seek a better life for himself far away from his failures. Because, what was there for him, when his parents were long departed and his other family members scattered all over the country? He had to leave. In our years together, I met members of Sizwe's family at various events: Mvula's baptism, Easter holidays, funerals of cousins and aunts and uncles. We winced, and laughed privately at relatives who asked us, eyes heavy with expectations: "So, when are you two jumping the broom, heh?" They came to our house, and Ma, on her best behaviour, welcomed them. No one spoke of his wife. No one spoke of his boy child.

"I'm such an idiot." I withdraw my hand from his grip and stand, almost knocking him over. But my legs are stubborn and won't let me move. I sit back down on the edge of the sofa.

"Let me help you up," Sizwe says, extending his hand.

"No, don't." I shove his hand away. "What is she doing here? What are they doing here?"

"She wants me to go back home. I told her my life is here, home is here with you. Anele, I'm sorry."

"You must stop apologising, okay? Just stop. Be my woman, be my woman, that's what you said. Be my woman. Meanwhile you have a woman! I don't know what to say to you." I am beginning to feel I might cry.

"You have every right to be angry with me. Know that nothing changes, I love you. I love you with all my heart. I'm here for you and Mvula. I'm here for us."

I steady myself up and switch off the television. "I don't know what hurts me most, you lying about your marriage or hiding the fact that you had a child or your cowardice. Is that what you do when things get rough, walk away?"

"No, no, I made a mistake. Anele, I swear on my mother and father's graves, she never told me about the child. Do you think I would turn my back on my own flesh and blood?"

"I don't know what to think right now, Sizwe, I must go. I must go. My sister is dead, *my* family needs me."

I shove the remaining unfolded clothes in the washing baskets and drag them out of the house.

"Let me help," Sizwe offers.

"No!"

"Anele, please, can we talk about this?"

"No, go be with your wife. I have nothing to say to you."

Sizwe's wife and child have climbed back into his car. Their eyes follow us as I hurry towards my car, Sizwe trailing behind me like a puppy.

I dump the laundry in the back seat, and once seated behind the steering wheel, turn to him. "You can't stay here. I don't want you here."

Sizwe's anguish is written all over his face. He is quiet for a minute, and then he says, "I understand. I hope you accept that I never meant to hide the truth from you. I regret that with all my heart." He glances up at me as though I will suddenly change my mind, tell him he can't go be with his family, that he belongs with us too. "Anele, I want to be with you."

"No, you can't be with me. How?" I'm screaming. "You have already chosen, remember? You committed to someone, for better or worse. No, I don't think so. It's too late for us. You must go now."

"I'm not giving up on you. I will fix this mess, I promise. I'm not giving up on you."

I reverse out of the yard.

Sizwe runs towards the car shouting, "Anele, please. Anele –"

"You must be gone tomorrow. I mean it."

I drive, and drive, until, with mist in my eyes, I notice the clock on the dashboard and turn around and go to my sister's house.

redemption

Fikile's body arrives in a white funeral car with white flags flanking its sides. Mbuso and Auntie Ntombi's cars follow slowly behind, hazards flashing. A small group of family and friends and strangers have gathered near the gate, singing church hymns in controlled sombre voices. They erupt into fits of hysteria when the procession passes through, fresh grief fills the air as if Fikile has just died.

From Lesihle's bedroom, I watch the driver of the hearse and his assistant jump out of the car and place Fikile's coffin on the stretcher, and with Auntie Ntombi's instructions, wheel her inside the house. Thiza's mother and Auntie Betty emerge from the hearse, followed by Ma, whose limp body threatens to tumble under the pressure of heartache. Auntie Betty links her arm under her sister's shoulder, and with the help of Uncle Majaha, pushes her towards the house. It is a scene I witnessed at my father's funeral. I had watched my mother's legs cave in and her body collapse on the ground when they brought his body home. When she came to, after Auntie Betty dabbed a damp cloth on her forehead and made her drink sugar water, she got to her feet, went straight to the closed coffin – the undertakers had recommended the family not view the body due to the severity of the injuries – bashed and screamed at the wood as though her dead husband would suddenly wake up and apologise for the confusion. It took three grown men to subdue and move her away from the coffin. Someone gave her pills that made her sleep throughout the wake and the night. When she woke up the following morning, she washed and dressed, and moved around like her husband had not died. My mother buried our father without shedding a tear. When the funeral was over, the last of the pots cleaned and relatives gone, leaving the silence, she went to sleep and never really woke up.

Mbuso does not leave his car. He sits, his head hunched over the steering wheel. At our father's funeral, Mbuso was restless, screaming for Ma. He had cried, gnawed at my thighs until Ma saw him and motioned that I bring him to her.

I watch the procession as if the coffin is carrying someone I vaguely know – a neighbour from three streets away, a distant grandmother I last saw when I was twelve, someone I only knew by name – and not my sister. Soon I will join in the mourning; strangers will search my face and try to make eye contact to assure me I'm not alone, one is never alone in this. Friends and family will cling onto me, weeping into my neck, screaming Fikile's name, their warm tears soaking my dress until I too burst out. Fikile would have hated everything about the moment.

For now, I leave the room and busy myself with the task of looking for the children. I seek the distraction of their tiny laughter, indolent talk of school and best friends, minor complaints and accusations among themselves, and questions I will struggle to find satisfactory responses to. I find them at the back of the house eating a large bag of cheese puffs. More than a dozen nieces and nephews, some whose names I haven't memorised, some too young to understand why they are exiled to the back and bribed with chips.

"Look what Daddy bought us," Mvula says, dipping into the bag and scooping a handful, to the dissatisfaction of the others, and shoving them to me. Her mouth has turned orange from the colouring. "Want some? They are really nice."

I shake my head, not wanting to think of Sizwe who had brought the treat. "I'm fine, baby, thank you." I walk over to Lesihle, seated on the grass on the edge of the fence, away from the *children*, "Where is your older brother?"

Lesihle shrugs violently. Her tiny body heaves up and down as if in rhythm with the growing noise in the front of the house. I perch myself next to her, feeling the softness of the grass on my bum, and let her weep on my lap for a while.

"It's unfair. Why does it have to be my mother?" Lesihle says, still face down. "She didn't do anything wrong, she was a good mother."

"I'm sorry." I cannot offer more to Lesihle, who now looks at me, eyes red and teary and expectant. I can't tell her it's the way of the world, not now anyway. "I'm sorry."

I rock Lesihle until her hiccups subside.

"I can never replace your mother, nobody can, but I will always be here for you and your brothers. You are my children now, okay?"

227

Lesihle nods.

"I must find Khanya; do you know where he is?"

"In Uncle Sizwe's car," Lesihle says quietly.

"Will you make sure they don't eat too many of those?" I gesture at the children.

I find Khanya and Vuma inside the car, Vuma behind the steering wheel and Khanya in the front passenger seat, so preoccupied with their cell phones they don't see me approach. The radio is turned off. They both straighten up and put the phones down when I poke my head inside the window.

"Can I join you for a minute?"

Khanya nods.

I slide into the back seat, put my feet up.

Vuma says he is thirsty and leaves to get water.

"How are you?"

"Fine, I guess," Khanya says.

The procession has moved inside the house; the noise is faint from where we are seated.

"I know it's not easy for you."

"I want this whole thing to end. I'm sick of the misery, Mom is dead and is not coming back. We must accept that."

"People deal with heartache in different ways. We must allow them to grieve and celebrate your mother in their own way."

He starts fidgeting with his hands.

"What is it?"

"I did not say goodbye to Mom, I should have been at home."

"Oh, Khanya, nobody said goodbye, and I was with her every day. We hoped she would come around as she had done many times before."

"I miss her, Aunt."

"You know she loved you, till the very end. Even when she struggled to breathe or speak properly, she never once forgot to ask after you and your brother and sister. I want you to remember that."

"What will happen with Dad, is he going to take another wife?"

I shift slightly to adjust my body. I catch Khanya's eyes in the rear-view mirror. "Why do you ask?"

"I don't think Dad cares that Mom is gone," he says in the nonchalant manner teenagers have when concealing hurt and anger.

"That is not a way to talk about your father, Fikile raised you better than that."

"He didn't love Mom. He told her many times to her face. He once said he wished she was dead. Ma laughed and brushed it off the way she always dismissed things like they were not true or unimportant or would go away."

I conjure Fikile's face during that moment, deeply embarrassed by the knowledge that her eldest child had heard his father wishing death upon her.

"I understand your anger and frustration but you're wrong about your father. He loved your mother very much."

"You don't have to protect him, that was Mom's job."

Khanya is laying a trap and I know it. "Okay, young man, that's enough. I will not tolerate you talking about your parents this way. You are a child, what do you know? Your father is inside right now paying his respects to his wife –"

"Well it's too late for him to show remorse. He had plenty of time to do that when Mom was alive."

"One day you will grow up and understand how life works."

We sit in silence.

"Are you going to force us to stay with him?"

"No, I mean, I don't know. Thiza is your father, he is responsible for you."

"I'm sorry, Aunt, but I will not stay with him and you can't force me to."

"Look, can we deal with one thing at a time? Can we lay your mother to rest first? Can we do that?"

Khanya nods.

"Thank you," I say and get out of the car. Khanya has left me exhausted. I want to sleep. I want to cry. I start to walk towards the gate, out into the darkening streets. In a moment, the family will be called to view the corpse. We will file in a line and one by one take a peek at Fikile's body for the last time. Afterwards, while peeling the hard shells of butternuts and wiping tears from onion sting, we will discuss how childlike Fikile looked in the coffin as if it wasn't her at all. I decide I will not see my dead sister's body, I prefer to remember her as she was, full of life, and not a

230

waxy statue in make-up and a bright blue lace dress. I wonder if the dress had been a gift from Sello.

* * *

The evening service of the wake is in full swing when I return. Inside the red-and-white tent, erected in front of the house, people take turns to stand and talk about Fikile the way they knew her, her generosity. In between the speakers and testimonies, the youth choir from her church clap and tap and stomp the ground. For a moment, the coffin and Fikile's body thawing inside is forgotten. Reverend Madida has respected the wishes the deceased left for the living to carry out, the service is joyous – as Fikile would have wanted it.

When the service is over, The Ladies of Vuka MaAfrica Society assemble at the back of the house by the kitchen. They put on pinafores and aprons, lay foldable steel tables, take out sharpened knives from their bags, and big bowls and pots, and start peeling and chopping vegetables. They cut the meat, fresh slaughter blood still dripping, into smaller pieces for the stew. There are about a dozen of them plus a few family members who have come out to assist. They work like a lean machine, only pausing to wipe tiny beads of sweat from their foreheads, squash mosquitoes and bat away moths, clap their hands, or sip on ice-cold drinks stored in coolers under the tables.

Khanya finds me here, a big head of cabbage in my hand. Auntie Betty says I should take a break, she fears I will collapse from exhaustion. I haven't stopped moving since Fikile died, the alternatives are not enticing – forcing sleep when I know none will come or sitting in the lounge with the old folks listening to them discuss swollen feet and incontinence, Fikile's coffin looming large in the corner of the room. I tell her I prefer to help.

"Dad wants to talk to you, he's in his car," Khanya whispers.

"Tell him I'll be there in a minute." I put the cabbage down and leave my space at the chopping table. I go over to the sink, wash my hands and the knife, and put it in the pocket of my apron, before hurrying towards the gate where Thiza is parked. The yard is a hive of activity, there is a roar of laughter, deep laughter, and talk coming from the side of the garage where a small fire burns and a smell of roasting meat wafts our way. A small group sits not too far from the fire, and pass around Auntie Betty's sorghum beer in plastic jugs.

I bump into Mbuso as I turn the corner. I tell him Thiza has called for me.

"To talk about what?"

"I don't know."

"Will you be okay, should I come with you?"

"No, I'll be fine."

I find Thiza inside his car, sitting in the dark. I walk over to the driver's side, stand a foot away from the car. "You want to see me," I say, slightly out of breath.

Thiza opens the door and steps out. His body is half hidden from the dull glow coming from the tent so that I only see his silhouette. I'm reminded of the time when he was still courting Fikile, how he used to come to our house in the evenings and park his car under the same tree, while Fikile blushed and jerked her head sideways to check if any of our neighbours were watching through the windows. Thiza never wore his work clothes when he came, he was in tracksuits or shorts or jeans, and appeared like any boy. Once, spying through the curtain, I saw Thiza grab her wrists – Fikile hesitant at first – and adjust her to face him and kiss her for what seemed to take forever. I must have let out a sound because Ma, in slumber on the sofa, opened her eyes and asked what was wrong. Some minutes later Fikile came in smiling and licking her lips and said I had to up my snooping game because she saw me peeping through the small crack of the curtains. This was the day she became Thiza's girlfriend.

"Tomorrow I will bury my wife, whom I loved," Thiza says not taking his eyes off me. "A wife who loved me unconditionally, was on my side through thick and thin, when no one believed in me. A wife who blessed me with beautiful and healthy children."

I don't say anything.

"I know you hate me, your family hates me. I know you think I was cruel to your sister, didn't treat her well. I see how your brother looks at me as if I'm a piece of shit. Let me tell you something, I was the one who pulled this family out the ditch. When you had nothing, not even a slice of bread or teaspoon of sugar in the house, who bought groceries? Me. Who kept the lights on? Put clothes on your backs? Me." He beats his chest as he says this. "And what did your precious Mbuso do when he had a chance to uplift his family? He ran away, hid behind education, and completely neglected your mother. Now he prances around like some hot shot because he wears a tie to work and drives a fancy car. He thinks he can look down on me."

I consider my response before I speak. "Thiza, there are mounds of vegetables waiting to be peeled. What do you want?"

"You all act like I'm the monster. You act as if Fikile was pure, not capable of any wrongdoing."

"I'm sorry, Thiza, but I don't have time for this. I've got work to do."

"She was not a saint."

"I know she was not a saint, but Fikile would not have left you to die on your own. How many times did you visit her while she was dying and needed you? Do you want me to count for you? How do you think that made her feel? How often did you come to check on the children? Do you think they didn't miss their father? What do you think they were eating, Thiza? Air? I'm not going to stand and listen to your sob story while you were never present when it mattered. And as for you taking care of us, maybe you did buy us bread and sugar, but my sister paid more than a thousandfold with her loyalty and kindness to you. So, please do me a favour and never speak to me about how you lifted us out of poverty. Never, ever!" I'm aware of the violence in my voice.

"Your mother wanted Fikile and the children to move back with you, and now it's my fault? How? You see this is what I mean, your family blames me for everything."

"Because what were you going to do for them had they stayed with you? Wasn't it your wife who told us she is relying on Lesihle because you were busy playing husband in another man's house? Did you expect us to fold our hands and watch Fikile suffer? You humiliated her, Thiza. You wouldn't even help her clean up after herself. In a way, I'm glad my sister is dead and spared from living this heartache."

I turn to walk away and find Mbuso standing behind me.

"Is everything okay?"

"Yes, we're finished here. Unless you still want to say something, Thiza."

"That time you found us, she wouldn't let me touch her," Thiza says. "She was too embarrassed for me to see her that way, helpless and dirty. She asked me to leave. And I did. I left the house to give her privacy. I wasn't running away."

It happened in Fikile's house, a week or so before Fikile moved in with us permanently. I was on my way to work when I decided to stop in and see her. The children had left for school. I let myself in through the kitchen door as usual.

"Fikile?" I called out her name, as I moved from the kitchen to her bedroom.

"Please go away!" I heard Fikile's voice. Thiza suddenly appeared around the corner and almost knocked me over.

"What's going on? Why is Fikile crying?" I asked him but he was already outside the door leading to the garage. I heard him enter his car, the garage door opening, and the car reversing out. I ran to their bedroom and found Fikile coiled on the bathroom floor, her underwear soiled.

"I'm like a child, I can't even make it to the toilet. I want to die now. Please, God, let me die."

Thiza looks at Mbuso and I and starts to shake his head. "I loved your sister. I want you both to know that."

I don't say anything because I know he did, at least he once did, stupidly and madly, even sacrificed his marriage for Fikile, made a home with her.

"And I love my children. I will never walk away from my children's lives the way my father disappeared from mine."

Thiza leaves us and walks towards where the men are seated.

"What was that about?" Mbuso asks.

"Something that should have happened months ago. Thiza wants redemption. He doesn't want to carry the burden of being the person who brought so much misery to Fikile's life. He is putting this as a challenge to me, I guess, to protect him, speak on his behalf. He has been persecuted, he believes, it's his way of saying: I'm tired, I don't want to fight. I want a truce."

"If he stops behaving like an asshole, maybe we will take him seriously."

"He is trying, Mbuso."

I resume my place at the chopping table, and after a few minutes put my knife down, and head to the bedroom. I lie down in bed, fully clothed, and close my eyes. Sleep comes immediately.

❧

the people of new hope know
how to do funerals

I have been anticipating this moment since the day my sister told me Doctor Thusi had found a lump on her left breast. I never thought it possible for one to experience a myriad of conflicting feelings at the same time. I am furious that the cancer lodged itself in my sister's perfectly healthy body, feasted, and left it lifeless. I am furious that I carry the fear of our future in my breath, my voice, my strides. I look at Ma and know I could never leave her. But I am relieved that my sister is dead, that I can finally swallow the bitter lump wedged in my throat all those years, just waiting.

I think of Fikile's illness as a monster freak storm, the thing that comes and destroys and alters everything along its path, the thing that forces one to reprioritise and rebuild. There were days when Fikile's cancer did not exist in my mind, days when I went to work and joined the office born-agains who prayed for my sister in the open morning prayer because, as Ma said, Fikile needed all the positive wishes she could get, drafted budgets that were always overspent, and dealt with irate procurement officers who stormed my office demanding explanations for unprocessed supplier payments. "This is how we kill small businesses in this country, and then wonder why the economy remains stagnant," they would snap accusingly. Days when I strolled to the nearby park with Eunice and sat on the bench and ate leftovers and dabbled in office gossip and lamented the cost of frozen chicken pieces and bread, and later when I went home fixed dinner, climbed into bed and made passionate love to Sizwe, which left him gasping for air and falling asleep wearing a stupid smile on his face. Those were the days when I spoke to Fikile, our chats standard, trivial even. I told her about passing my exams and the three modules standing between me and my Master's degree, Mvula's new favourite expression, a leaking toilet that Sizwe had finally fixed, and new television dramas that held me gripped and missing bedtime.

Fikile in turn filled me in on Lesihle's latest revolt – "She is becoming impossible, I have to catch myself from smacking that silly pout of hers. Were we like this in our adolescent years?" – the impossibility of the paperwork to access government funding for her preschool, her declining sex drive and how she's not bothered in any way – "Thiza has not even noticed because he's getting plenty from his *hoochies*." Afterwards I'd hang up and sit with Ma and we would have sweet Rooibos tea with lemon.

Other times the pain resurfaced, fresh and sharp as a knife's edge. On those days, I wept for my sister. There was no pattern to the explosions, no forewarning – realising we were out of bread or milk in the morning, a smiling bride on a magazine cover, a scene on the evening news – and within seconds, I would be reduced to torrents of uncontrollable tears. I noticed I was not the only one susceptible to these emotions, Bafana experienced them too. He would, without provocation, start crying for his mother. He would sit by himself, sucking his thumb, a habit we all thought he had outgrown but came back as Fikile's condition worsened. There was no appeasing him, and so we left him to cry until he fell asleep. Ma cried for Fikile every night when she prayed and every morning when she woke up. If Lesihle cried, she did so privately.

Fikile did not volunteer information about her illness. I dug. I wanted to know what it was like, what she felt knowing that her body was walking around with enemy cells, that the good cells would one day decide to pack up and not to put up the fight anymore. I begged my sister to describe her pain as if it would rub off on me, and somehow my super cells would attack, obliterate and defeat the disease. In the years Fikile lived with cancer – a time spent drugged with morphine, sitting under chemo or under the knife – I was once seriously ill with flu from a boil infection I had left untreated for too long. The pus had spilled into my bloodstream and wreaked havoc. The doctors drained the boil and put me on antibiotics.

The first Sunday after her diagnosis, Fikile asked me to go to church with her. I expected her to weep to God and demand answers, or rise from her seat, arms flailing, and beg Reverend Madida to bless her and cast away the devil eating up her body. I expected her to bellow to the congregation and ask them to pray for her. Instead Fikile prayed quietly next to me and when the service was over, stayed behind for a few minutes exchanging hugs with other members, her face plastered in a brave smile.

It's a terrible thing to say I'm relieved Fikile's journey has come to an end, to say I did not expect Fikile to live for as long as she did. I know the exact moment I first let hope drain out of me. And after that, each time she came down with something – a headache that throbbed for days threatening to blow her brains out, a bruise that refused to heal, shortness of breath – I said to Sizwe: "This is the end, I don't see how she will overcome this." Truth is, I have been burying my sister for years.

*   *   *

I wake up to Sizwe's gentle shake. He is leaning over, calling my name. We have managed to stay out of each other's way since that afternoon at Ma's. I have observed him from afar, and take pleasure in the subtle hostility Eunice channels towards him. I do not ask if he has moved out of my mother's house. Sizwe tells me Ma insisted I sleep until just before the service starts.

"We will get through this," he says, stroking my face with his hand. "I'll make you happy, I promise."

I watch him leave the room before I slip out of bed and run a quick bath. I dress in clothes I have decided to burn after the funeral. When I emerge from the bedroom, I'm assaulted by heavy scents of musk and lavender and baby powder. The house is an abrupt mess. The hallway is littered with mattresses, blankets, pillows, clothes and shoes. Everyone has left for church.

I walk over to the kitchen to find mountains of dirty cups

and saucers, some with half-eaten scones and peanut butter sandwiches. I pick up a cup from the sink, rinse it, and make myself tea with plenty of sugar. My stomach growls but I can't force myself to eat. Lesihle comes in to tell me she will go to church with Sizwe and I.

"Who is with the kids?"

"Dad."

I ask her if she also wants tea.

"Okay," she says.

"Who chose your clothes?" She is wearing an unsuitably short sleeveless black dress, net stockings with butterflies, and high-heeled silver peep-toe sandals. These are not her clothes.

"Do you like my outfit?" She looks up brightly, innocently, impressed with her choice.

"I guess," I say, because now is not the time to tell her she looks a tad inappropriate for a thirteen-year-old attending a funeral.

"Cousin Thuli said I could keep the dress if I like. Can I?"

"I think Thuli was being nice, and didn't mean for you to *keep, keep* it."

"She said it's too small for her anyway. She said she will give it to someone else if I don't want it."

"We will talk about the dress later, Lesihle, okay?"

We sit and drink our tea in silence.

"Remember the time you, me, and your mom went to that coffee shop in town by the botanical gardens and ordered cappuccinos for us and hot chocolate for you, and ate cake?"

"Yeah, I had the best chocolate cake ever."

"Yes, the cake was moist and absolutely mouth-watering. Your mother's crèche performed well that year and for the first time since she opened. She was so proud that she could afford to pay the teachers' salaries in full and on time. I was thinking maybe after the funeral you and I should go back there. Would you like that?"

Lesihle nods.

"Your mother was sick, you saw her. Doctors tried everything they could to save her life, and we prayed for her. It was her time to leave us. You know she is in a better place now?"

"I know, Auntie."

We finish our tea. Balancing precariously on the borrowed heels, Lesihle takes the cups and negotiates her way to the sink. I cover my mouth to stop myself from laughing.

"Are you sure you don't want to wear your normal shoes?"

"Yes."

I stand, take her hand, and we walk to the car where Sizwe is waiting. As we are getting in, I receive a text message on my phone. It is from Sello Mabe, telling me that he is thinking of us and apologising for not being able to attend the funeral. I turn my phone off and put it away. I don't speak to Sizwe.

When we arrive, we hear the youth church choir hum in a slow tempo. The coffin stands at the front of the church, draped in a heavy purple and white blanket – one of Fikile's. On top is an arrangement of wreaths. We take the nearest available seats. From where we sit, I see Ma and Thiza's mother, and my aunts' bodies rise and fall to the melody of agony. Lesihle starts to heave to the trance, I pull her close. I see Thiza's bald head in the front row, bowed, Bafana sitting on his lap facing the back, towards the congregation. He sees us, jumps off his father's lap and comes running straight to mine.

"Where were you all this time?" he demands.

"*Shh*, Bafana, the minister is going to start preaching," Lesihle hisses.

I look at her and smile.

The people of New Hope know how to do funerals. Three other people will be buried today, young people like my sister who had their whole lives ahead of them. There is no escaping the relentlessness of disease and death for us. People I grew up with have been wiped out as if by a cruel famine. A few years back, I and a few high school classmates had unexpectedly gathered at a local shisanyama. It was during the Easter break, people I had not seen in years, fortunate people who had escaped the clutches of our town, returned briefly home. Delirious with nostalgia, alcohol, and scourging heat, someone had suggested a reunion for our matric class at the end of the year. For a moment the idea was tossed around. Yes, wouldn't it be nice to gather the matric class? Yes, it would be great to reconnect. That was until someone, jokingly, pointed out that the group, as we were, was all that was left of our class. There was no one else to invite. We were having a reunion.

The residents have come out early and in respectable numbers to help us lay Fikile to rest. A normal Saturday morning, with people to bury, people to wed, stokvels and braais to attend later. It will be all over by noon; the tent will be folded in a heap and plastic chairs stacked in rows ready for collection, pots washed, dishes, glasses and cutlery counted, mourners dispersed, and the grieving family left to wash down its sorrows with tea and ice-cold drinks and beer. Inside the house, the furniture will be rearranged, Fikile's mattress returned to her bedroom, the blankets washed and drenched in fabric softener, and the television turned on in time for the evening programmes. Life restored.

The funeral programme calls for a few people to relive their memories of Fikile, someone speaking on behalf of each of the families – the maternal side, paternal side, the Dlamini family – on behalf of friends, on behalf of neighbours. I look around and see a haze of familiar faces, people dabbing tissues and wiping their eyes, their faces swollen with ache. Uncle Joseph is seated at the back. He nods when our eyes meet. Sizwe joins his brother and his sister-in-law seated a couple of rows behind my family. My eyes instantly scan the crowd for Sizwe's wife and the boy, I do not see them; I don't know why I think they would be here and what I would do if they are here. My colleagues have shown up in their numbers. Eunice and her husband and kids are seated not too far from us. Her lips ask, "Are you okay?" I smile and nod. Fikile's friend Nikiwe is here too. She weeps silently into her handkerchief. I turn to my right and spot

Nolwazi. She has brought her son, same age as Bafana, and Khanya's spitting image. Fikile knew about the child. She had just started her first course of chemotherapy when she discovered Thiza's affair: "Bastard has done it again," was all she said. We never told Ma; if my aunts knew, they never said anything. Nolwazi nods and mimes something resembling an apology one shares with the aggrieved. I stare at her while I draw Bafana closer and kiss the back of his head. You're not the only winner here, Fikile was not a fool after all. I want to scream at her. Nolwazi turns her face away from me and looks straight ahead.

Khanya reads his mother's obituary with clarity and purpose. He has his mother's spirit, not easily frightened. He had asked to write the obituary, perhaps his way of saying goodbye. He apologised then for his behaviour in the car. We sat, me, him, Mbuso and Vuma, and attempted to compress Fikile's life into a single piece of paper. I mostly narrated the significant events, with Mbuso contributing what he knew or thought he remembered. I was filled with a strange elation watching the astonishment in my brother's face as I weaved through my sister's life, moments he had no memory of, no place in. When I was finished, Vuma helped Khanya with grammar and checked his spelling. Khanya read the passage out loud to Ma and my aunts. We were all pleased; Fikile had lived a complete life. Mbuso emailed the document to the funeral undertakers.

Lesihle and one of her cousins take turns to read the cards with the flowers and wreaths stacked by the coffin.

Reverend Madida delivers a poignant sermon on the stages of grief. When he is finished, I think I hear Fikile's voice say Amen.

* * *

We bury Fikile in one of the three open graves under a giant fever tree. The other two funerals are already in the grave-yard when we arrive, metres away from us. The three pro-gramme directors coordinate the proceedings like policemen at a busy road intersection. It is a spectacular moment. The mourners are cordial to each other, united in pain and song and dust. We go back and forth, steadily moving through the programmes, until all three coffins are lowered. This too is not an anomaly.

I look up from where I'm seated under the small tent re-served for family, and see Mapule in the crowd. I blink and look again because I do not trust the fog in my eyes. It is her. She is wearing a large black hat to shield her from the tormenting sun. She sees me looking and smiles. I smile back and turn to my brother seated behind me. I find an empty chair. Mbuso has moved to join my uncles and cousins and other local men filling Fikile's grave with soil. One of the men hands him a shovel, he scoops the soil from a small heap next to the grave and pours it into the hole. My brother looks out of place doing this but he is determined. He scoops and pours the earth into Fikile's grave until another man taps his shoulder and takes the shovel from him. Mbuso steps back and wipes the sweat off his forehead.

He stands there with the men until they have filled the hole to the top.

The people around me start to move away from the graves towards their cars, I stand but find I cannot move. My chest floods with sudden sadness, I feel my legs separate from the rest of my body. Mbuso sees me, and grabs me by my shoulders as I'm going down. He lowers me onto a chair. Khanya brings me a bottle of water.

We are the last to leave: Mbuso, Khanya, Lesihle and I. I tell the children to know where their mother is, that they can always come here to talk to her. No one is crying, and I'm relieved.

Mapule appears behind us. After a slight hesitation, Mbuso walks over to her. They embrace for the longest time. Mbuso holds her hand and leads her to me and the children.

"I'm sorry," Mapule whispers.

We hug and return home without Fikile.

Later we are sitting on the veranda. The white tent stands erect in the yard, folded trestle tables line the wall, and black plastic chairs are stacked up awaiting collection. It is just us now, family and a few friends; Fikile's absence is evident, raw. Ma comes out to join us. Her walk is slow and unbalanced, she looks as if she may not make the short distance to us. I notice how grief has aged her; her skin has become dull and lifeless, cheeks prominent and sharp, and the stubborn dark rings make her eyes look vacant. She has lost weight too; her new dress, although her size, hangs loose off her shoulder.

We stop talking for a second, eyes shifting to the bucket full of drinks and alcohol in front of us, too late to hide it. We do this all the time, though Ma has been sober for years now. We laugh nervously afterwards, consumed with guilt and suspicion, and promise to trust her a little more. I know the edginess and fear of a relapse will never stop, a feeling that keeps me awake at night.

Ma does not even glance at the bucket. She talks to us about rituals to be observed including distributing Fikile's clothes among family members. Ma refused to get rid of my father's clothes for years after his death, every few months she emptied his wardrobe, taking out each item and laying it on the bed. She would cry as she folded and hung the clothes back in their place. One day Ma phoned Uncle Majaha and asked him to come and take his brother's clothes. She folded the clothes into big plastic bags and left them in the lounge for him. When he came, two weeks later, she told him to do whatever he thought best, that he was the only person she trusted with her husband's clothes.

Sizwe loiters around for a moment, and eventually finds a way to keep himself busy transporting the remaining relatives to the bus and taxi rank. Mapule leaves shortly after, it's a long drive back home, she says.

"You will come back to visit us?" I ask.

"Of course, I will." She squeezes my hand.

Mbuso walks her to her car.

I wait until the last of the relatives and friends have left to tell Mbuso about my visit with Sello Mabe. My brother listens with his head sideways, and when I'm finished, rubs his eyes.

"Oh, Fikile," he says, defeated.

"Sello spoke of his desire to tell his truth while he has a chance. I've been trying to peel the layers of our conversation for signs that he may take matters into his own hands, announce himself to our family as Fikile's lover: 'Hello, my name is Sello Mabe. I've come to claim what's mine.'"

"Would he?"

"I don't know. He doesn't strike me as a man who stirs and then leaves things unfinished. He will come for his son."

"We don't know if he is the father."

"That thought crossed my mind, except why would he lie?"

"It's too soon," Mbuso says. "I hope he is decent enough to respect that we're in mourning. He must understand the delicacy of the matter and that it will take time to resolve."

"I can't imagine telling Ma, let alone Thiza."

We agree to leave the matter as is, for now, at least, because what else can we do with a deceased woman's secret?

a new normal

Three days after we bury Fikile we gather our belongings in bags and laundry bins and boxes and make the pilgrimage back to our mother's house, leaving Thiza alone with his memories. Auntie Betty has decided to stay with us until the New Year. She and Ma have settled into a comfortable routine of early morning tea, watching reruns of television soapies, keeping the children occupied before the schools open and guarding them against eating too many sweets and upsetting their stomachs. The children have already endured the first dose of Epsom salts, which left them scrambling for the toilet one after another. Auntie Betty did the same when my father died, uprooted her life into ours, and for weeks offered herself to us unreservedly. She watched her sister coming undone, and wept at her own helplessness and failure to right the situation.

Auntie Ntombi stops by often. The divorce has not taken away her sense of humour. She smiles and cracks dry jokes about how she has Uncle Joseph by the balls, and that her victory is certain. She says as soon as her money comes, she will take us all on a holiday by the sea for a week because God knows we deserve it. Mbuso says he supports the notion and pledges to help our aunt.

Khanya spends his time hanging around his uncle. I sometimes eavesdrop on their conversations about the looming matric year, girls – yes, he sort of has someone or two but it's nothing serious – and architecture, his career of choice, and the universities he will be applying to. I notice how his choices have changed considerably to be those closer to his uncle.

I have not yet felt the hollowness of adjusting to a life without my sister with the house still so full of people. We talk about her all the time as if stopping would wipe out her memory forever. Sometimes the conversations are peppered with stiff silences followed by short nervous sighs. The other day at breakfast, Bafana looked up from his bowl of oatmeal and with a straight face said to Ma: "Is my mother not coming to eat? Is she not hungry?"

"Aunty is in heaven, don't you know?" Mvula responded without missing a beat.

I held my breath expecting an outburst, expecting Bafana to rubbish his cousin's response and demand a real answer. Instead he said, "I knew that," and returned to his meal.

Fikile's children's hair has been shaved off and buried at the back of their house. Thiza and us, close family, wear a small square black cloth on our sleeves to symbolise our loss. After a month, a goat will be slaughtered and the family cleansed, and we will then be able to move on with our lives.

Mbuso has not left nor has he said anything about his plans. I suspect my brother is aware of his place in our lives. He tackles each day with tenacity, and with what we sometimes read as permanency. But we still hold our breath, our hearts beat in anticipation of his announcement to

258

return to his life, a life excluding us. Ma told me she will never forgive herself if Mbuso leaves us again, that she couldn't bear to lose another child, to death or life. I told her she was unreasonable to put such a responsibility on herself, that Mbuso was old enough to make his own choices. She sighed, said that's how she felt about it, and I wouldn't know because Mbuso is not my child.

One afternoon I saw Ma walk into Mbuso's room. She was inside for a while, and when she came out, she was wiping her eyes with the hem of the black shawl which she had taken to wearing since my sister's death. Mbuso emerged a few minutes later, his eyes bloodshot and glassy.

True to his word, Mbuso went with Khanya and Bafana to clean Fikile's yard. They woke up a few days after the funeral and loaded garden tools in his car and set off. Later Khanya showed me the "before" and "after" pictures of the lawn. They had removed all the overgrown ivy, mowed the grass which had grown knee length in some areas, and replaced the wilted marigolds with succulents. Ma looked at the pictures and said Fikile would be proud. At home, Mbuso has organised people to repaint the exterior of our house when the New Year starts. This pleases Ma.

Mapule calls. She promises to visit soon. "That is, if your brother allows me," she adds hastily. I tell her she can visit us anytime she chooses, "Mbuso is not a boss of our relationship with you." Mapule packs out laughing, says she will make a plan. I ask Mbuso if they are talking again. He gives me that lopsided smile of his, and says yes but warns I shouldn't read too much into anything. He says he is not in a rush for a relationship.

"I'm loving my space, and importantly, I'm loving connecting with my people. When I think about how much of Fikile's life I missed out on, I know I can never be that person again. I'd be a proper fool to make the same mistake again. It is good to be home."

Because we are still bereaved, we limit our movements to show respect to our sister. People who have not yet shared their bereavement with us continue to visit. Ma sits with them on the Gommagommas. They read a verse and pray and drink juice and eat homemade biscuits if Auntie Betty has baked.

*　*　*

I will not take Sizwe's calls. I push away every memory of that afternoon as soon as it creeps into my mind. I don't trust myself to say what I need to say, or to constrain my tongue from lashing out what it shouldn't. I'm not ready for the regrets that will come afterwards. They say silence creates a vacuum – perhaps it is this vacuum I seek comfort in. I'm afraid of the blinding deception, I tell myself over and over that surely this can't be the worst thing Sizwe has done, that I'm outrageous to punish him this way. People walk away from people and the things they love all the time.

For now, I keep busy. Mbuso and I take the children out to a picnic at the park or to town to buy chocolate-dipped ice cream cones. I hide in my room or behind the boulders for hours at a time engrossed in books, new worlds I dream of, until my eyes are scratchy. Auntie Betty insists that I be left alone. I am polite to Sizwe when he is around, which is daily. I thank him for bringing fresh bread and milk and leafy spinach and butternut and plump tomatoes from the market on the main road and meat and sometimes cooked ground nuts and grilled corn which we devour until our jaws hurt. He checks around the house and I watch him laugh with Ma or share a beer with Uncle Majaha or a joint with Mbuso when they believe no one is watching.

Soon I run out of excuses explaining why he hasn't moved back in with us. "He still feels we need space as a family to get over our grief," I say. "Also, with Mbuso around, he is trying to navigate his place. Give him time."

"He can't be sleeping in the streets as if he does not have family," Ma retorts. "Tell him to come home immediately."

Auntie Betty looks at me and says nothing.

Sizwe's wife eventually opens the floodgate of deceit. She arrives one morning after breakfast. I'm drifting out of dreamy sleep on the sofa. In one dream, I'm with Fikile at the cemetery overlooking her grave. I ask her if she is happy, she smiles and says she doesn't know yet. I ask who she is with, and if she has seen Dad; she shakes her head.

I wake as Mvula comes to me heaving, "Ma, Ma, there's someone at the gate to see you."

"Who?"

"Aunty."

"Aunty who?"

She shrugs and runs back outside.

I drag myself off the sofa and out of the house.

Sizwe's wife smiles as I approach. "It's me, Pretty," she says.

"What do you want?" I demand, not returning the smile.

"Can we sit somewhere?"

I call for Lesihle to bring us two chairs. We sit under the tree. I remember my manners and ask Lesihle to get Pretty a drink.

"I am sorry. I didn't know Sizwe has another wife," she says.

"I'm not his wife."

"He lives with you and your family. He takes good care of you. To me you are a wife."

A thin silence.

"He was wrong not to tell you about us. He was very wrong. I am angry too." I notice a thin gold wedding band on her finger.

"Sizwe doesn't live here anymore."

After Lesihle skips off, I watch Sizwe's wife carefully pick up the glass and take a sip. She ignores the scones.

"I guess life is full of mysteries and surprises. I had dreams for us. Sizwe was my first, you see. I can't remember a time when I did not love that man, from when we were children in primary school fighting over who between the two of us runs faster, to high school, and after I left to study and came back, it was always Sizwe. We had a small wedding, only close family and friends, but it was beautiful. We were happy."

Pretty tells me how things changed after Sizwe lost his job at the construction company he had worked for since completing his apprenticeship as a young man. He considered those people his family, then one day they told him they were selling the company. He was shattered. He and a few of his co-workers tried to buy the business but were not able to raise the cash in time. Who would want to risk their money on a handful of workers with no notable business management skills? After searching for work for two years and surviving on piece jobs, he finally gave up. "I didn't make much but we could have survived until he found solid work. But no, his pride got the better of him. He felt if he couldn't take care of me, then he didn't deserve me. All nonsense of course, so I said no to the divorce. I couldn't give it to him, I still believed we could make us work; I never gave up on him," Pretty pauses, seems to catch some breath and then says in the most distraught tone, "The man left. Just left. I cannot begin to explain the hurt. He humiliated me in front of my family, his family, our friends. When I discovered I was expecting Mxolisi, I decided not to tell Sizwe, I guess that was my revenge. I've kept the boy from him until now. My sister, when you're consumed with anger, sometimes you take actions you may not necessarily be proud of later."

I should say something to this woman who has braved a journey of hundreds of kilometres to find her love and to fight for what she believes in. I should tell her about the hurt gnawing at my heart too, my own failings to see that my life with Sizwe has been *pretend*, like the children's game. I should tell her that she can have her husband back, that I do not believe I can forgive him. I swallow my words instead.

"Finally, here I am, I've come to show Sizwe his son. I have punished all of us enough now. I know I have lost him. I see the passion in his eyes when he speaks about you and your family. His heart is here. I am very sorry, Anele. Coming to New Hope, coming here today has been difficult for me, but it was important I speak to you. I'm very sorry about your sister."

Pretty swallows the last of her drink, thanks me and leaves as quietly as she came.

* * *

"Ushadile! Death always brings skeletons out of the closet, but this one takes the cup," Auntie Betty exclaims. I am downloading everything I know about my child's father and his secret world, words gush out of my mouth until I run out of breath and the hiccups come in successions.

"We can't say we're not disappointed with Mvula's father, but baby girl, this is not the end of the world," Auntie Ntombi says as she tries to force water down my throat to appease the hiccups. "You are a beauty. As soon as the whole of New Hope knows you're back in the market, you will be snatched up in no time. Just promise me to find someone with money this time. Don't go with only your heart, consider the wallet too."

I find myself laughing despite the disarray in my heart.

"No, no, no, don't burden Anele with this man talk," Auntie Betty retorts. "This child has been through a lot, she needs to clear her head and be ready for the mammoth task ahead of her. Men will only add stress to her life and cause her to lose focus."

"But she is young, Betty, she still has another shot at love."

"Aren't you too optimistic for someone going through a divorce?"

"I believe in love, Betty. Baby girl, don't listen to this one. She was burnt once and threw in the towel. Love is beautiful, and just because me and your uncle are calling it quits doesn't dictate the course of life for everyone. You will find your balance, you will find your soulmate."

Ma looks up at me as if considering a response, but decides against it. She loves Sizwe. Ma had steadily reduced her alcohol intake from the time Sizwe came into our lives. Each day I watched her take tiny bites of her food, chewing slowly like she was in pain. Doctor Thusi had warned her about the dangers of drinking on an empty stomach, particularly given her near-rotten liver, a call she never heeded until Sizwe showed up. Fikile and I spoke about this shift, how Ma was changing, her energy and life returning to her. Because we didn't believe that Ma could quit alcohol, on her own, we missed the moment when she completely stopped, shortly after Fikile was diagnosed the first time.

"Men have no truth," Aunty Betty says again, clapping her hands in defeat.

"You deserve better, sis," Mbuso says when we are alone. "But I respect whatever decision you make. You know Sizwe better than any of us."

"I don't know what I did wrong. You see what I mean about my life? It's like I'm stuck on a bad record shuffle."

* * *

I yield under the pressure of my own inner turmoil and give in to listening to Sizwe's lies or truths or whatever. We meet at a restaurant, away from the pressure of Ma's probing eyes as if I had brought shame on the family. We both order fizzy drinks, and ignore the food menus. I'm indifferent as he assures me that his wife, soon to be ex-wife, has finally agreed to the divorce, indifferent as he swears to become a present father to his son, indifferent as he promises to be the best husband and father to our daughter if I give him another chance. He was foolish, he knows better now, he says. Sizwe reaches for my face, searching for signs of reconciliation. He finds none.

"You are still angry. What can I do for you to forgive me?" His voice is soft and anxious.

"I don't know," I say because that is the truth.

"I can't live without you, Anele."

"I need time," I say in earnest. I don't tell Sizwe of the terrifying gap opening between us.

He looks up. "Okay, whatever time you need, I'll wait."

I rise to leave because all we needed to say is said.

"Anele, I didn't mean to hurt you, I'm sorry."

I leave Sizwe no wiser or closer to the answers I'm desperately seeking.

* * *

We celebrate Christmas at Auntie Ntombi's. We fill her house, me, Mbuso, the children, Ma, Auntie Betty, Uncle Majaha, and other cousins and their families. Even Thiza shows up shortly before we sit down for lunch. Ma personally calls Sizwe and invites him. When I protest, she tells me he is her guest, not mine. Mvula won't leave her father's side. She comes to me at the oddest times and asks with tears filling her small eyes when her father will be sleeping at home. "Soon, baby," I respond with a ready bribe, a sweet I fish out of my handbag or a promise of a movie. The presence of her cousins and uncle has helped buffer Sizwe's absence. For now, I buy another day. We sit around my aunt's extended table and stuff ourselves silly with Cornish chicken, lamb chops, roast honey-glazed butternut, and beetroot and feta salad – recipes Auntie Ntombi confesses she spent weeks practising after seeing them on television cooking shows. We take photos of the food and each other – wide, happy smiles for the camera. Auntie Ntombi says this is our new family tradition, she says from now on, we will always celebrate Christmas together. Uncle Majaha offers to host the following year, the women around the table exclaim in unison about the complication of the matter of who will cook.

"We will braai," my uncle says.

"No, Majaha, we don't want pap and vleis on Christmas. We want fancy foods, roast lambs and puddings."

"Ntombi, you like complicating things with your education."

"You can book a Christmas lunch at one of the hotels. Then we can braai at Uncle's the following day," Mbuso says.

"Now you're talking, my baby. You heard that, Majaha?"

We welcome the New Year at home. Mbuso buys several boxes of fireworks to the children's delight, and assists in lighting them at midnight. For a few minutes the location is a kaleidoscope of bright lights, noise and sulphur. Ma gathers us to pray for a good year and Fikile's safety and happiness. This is what a new normal is for us.

Thiza comes to see the children every few days, sometimes he takes them in his car to town and they return full and sleepy. Khanya makes a small effort to greet his father, but disappears soon after. Before the schools open in a couple of weeks, we will discuss a long-term arrangement for the children. Ma said Thiza would take the children over her dead body; I shudder to think of a life without my sister's children, but I leave room for disappointment. Thiza is their father. Mbuso and I don't speak about Bafana.

Sello Mabe sent another message saying he thought of our family often, that I should call him whenever I needed something, anything. I sent a text back thanking him. He did not ask about Bafana.

Once Ma caught me staring at Bafana.

"What is it?" she asked with that concerned look of hers.

268

"I have something to say," I said, my lips quivering. I tried to construct the sentence in my head but nothing came out. Ma was patient. After a while I said, "I don't know what's wrong with me."

"You are missing your sister," she said and squeezed my shoulder. "And that matter with Mvula's father, it can't be easy for you. In life we all make mistakes. I cannot tell you what to do, but Sizwe is a good man." Up until then Ma had not offered her opinion or openly chosen her allegiance.

"Ma, I don't know what good is anymore."

"You give up too easily, my child."

* * *

Ma and I visit Fikile's grave to remove the wilting flowers and to check that the granite slab with Fikile's name has not moved with the shifting soil beneath. We talk to Fikile, find out if she is settled. We fill her in on mundane talk about Bafana's endless jokes, on how Lesihle is slowly becoming a mother to all of us, like she just knows her role, and Khanya's drive and the gentleman he is turning out to be. We tell her how Mbuso is settling in and reclaiming his space in our lives, and how Mvula is happily basking in the attention of being the last born of the family. We move over to my father's grave at the bottom of the cemetery, and ask him to continue to protect us and Fikile.

* * *

Today I visit Fikile alone. I start with our normal routine and when I'm done polishing Fikile's tombstone, I lay down a blanket and sit at the foot of her grave, placing Sizwe's photograph next to me. I ask my sister after her health and if she is happy where she is. I ask her to guide me and to show me the way. Fikile was always the wise one, the one who took chances, the one who lived. She tackled everything head on and apologised and corrected mistakes later; for once I wish I was her. I love Sizwe but I don't know if love will heal my broken heart and make me trust him again.

I start to cry because this is Sizwe staring back at me with his earnest eyes and a full smile. Sizwe who has only been kind and compassionate and loving. Sizwe who was not turned off by the turmoil of disease and destruction that plagued my family for years. Sizwe, my daughter's father. I wait and wait and wait for an answer that I know will not come; I am not mad at my sister. A breeze passes and all is silent again.

Acknowledgements

I am thankful to everyone who made this book possible. In my research I read books and blogs, and watched numerous video journals by cancer survivors. I cried, and rejoiced with them when they achieved even the smallest milestones. I salute the many women who have been touched by cancer for their resilience and resolution to beat the disease, and for sharing their journeys with us. You are my heroes.

I don't have enough thank yous for my publisher, Carolyn Meads, for her meticulousness and allowing me time to collect my thoughts when I was in doubt. This book is truly ours. My editor, Zodwa Kumalo-Valentine, thank you for taking on this project. I'm grateful for the generous and honest reviews and guidance from anonymous readers and my friends, Angela Makholwa, Slindile Majola, Bongiwe Selane, Lindiwe Msiza, Diana Cumberledge and Mpho Mogotsi. To my family, my heart flows with only love for you.

NOZIZWE CYNTHIA JELE is a South African novelist. Her debut novel, *Happiness is a Four-Letter Word* (Kwela Books, 2010), has won numerous awards including the 2011 Commonwealth Writers' Prize in the Best First Book category (Africa region) and the 2011 M-Net Literary Award in the Film category. The film adaptation was released at the box office countrywide in February 2016. Nozizwe also writes short stories. She supports various initiatives to promote reading amongst young people, including The FunDza Literacy Trust.